AMIAYA ENTERTAINMENT LLC
Presents

All
or
Nothing

A NOVEL

by

Michael Whitby

Whitby

Officially Noted

Copyright ©2004 by Michael Whitby
Written by Michael Whitby for Amiaya Entertainment LLC
Published by Amiaya Entertainment LLC
Cover design by Marion Designs
Edited by Antoine "Inch" Thomas

Printed in the United States

ISBN: 0-9745075-7-1

[1. Urban-Fiction 2. Drama-Fiction 3. Philadelphia-Fiction]

5.00
6/18/08
NRN

Dedication

To my friend, my comrade, my brother

"BILLKWON."
You held me down through the best and worst of times and through the most important time...
Not the beginning or the end, but through all the struggle in between! That's when it counts!
You're "realness" personified...and that's gangsta!!

and,

To my mother, Cynthia Riddick! We've never seen eye to eye because we've been so caught up in this game, unwilling to lower our guards and be human.
It's alright to love each other because that's what a mother and son are supposed to do.
You exposed me to something that I've learned to *LOVE, HONOR, AND RESPECT*...... "this game." You made me strong and I love you always and forever!

Acknowledgements

First and foremost, I wanna thank everybody who kept me motivated and had faith in my ability to write. I wanna thank (Amiaya Entertainment) "Inch and Tania" for having that same faith by acknowledging my book. This is my very first legal venture so it means a lot to me. (Much Respect).

To my man FatherBorn from Patterson, NJ. You made it happen for me and real recognize real. Good looking!

To all my mans who couldn't be here... Bobby Smith, Tommy Ramirez, Larry Gross A.K.A 'Pep', Bad One, Ron G, Freaky Tah, Louis Colon.. Rest In Peace. I'll mourn you til I join you!

All my 2nd street souljas... stay focused strong and sucka free! Most importantly, stay free! And true to yourselves and this game! Don't be in the way when you can be on your way! (Real Rap) special shout outs to ...Billkwon, Mo' A.K.A Baby Don, Gee$ A.K.A The General, Antonia Mylnek, Ani-Dog, and those who matter. (You know if you do and if you don't).

To my baby brother "Jahaad"... Don't let anything break your spirit. Stay strong and know that although things seem to be at their worse, everything will work out for the best.

Joshua $ Jesus (My Brothers)... I Love you! that goes without question... Ocean City NJ...

To my grandmother "Iris Fennell" and my Auntie "Linda", my cousins... Merrill, Eshanda, Naderia, Naimah, Augustus, Rasool and Abdullaah...A.K.A John Rogers... (As-Salaam- Alaikum).

5

To all those who know someone who's locked down, don't find the time, make the time, to let them know they aint alone! A card, some flicks, money, letters, a visit goes a long way!

To those who read and can relate to or appreciate this book, spread the word, share the love and support "Amiaya Entertainment" because they represent the "Truth" told by those who love this shit... Peace!

To my mans and the few good brothers I had the opportunity to meet & know during my incarceration. "Shai" A.K.A Flatbush (Peace God), "D.Delacruz & Herm-Dog," (You the Realest), Jose "Zay" Quinonez (Holla At Ya Boy) Shannon Bates A.K.A Holiday. (Stay up Homie) Willie Blue and Moon (Good Looking). Peace Brother Beloved! J-5 & Tical Nitty, Dre, Will, Reese.. One Love!

To those I missed, it wasn't intentional. Holla at me, and I'll get you in the next one.

To Fancy, Shawn, Gutterman.. Keep writing and your time will come. Your talent is worthy of recognition. To my man Joe... "freecrazyjoe.com"

To Mrs. Kay Johnson and the Smith family, (Thank you!)

To my baby brother & sisters. Ebony, Driane, Laura, Gladys and "Matt-Matt"... I Love You.

Last but most definitely not least, to my "Victoria." Thanks for trying!

To all those that matter, Peace & Blessings!

"Tabat & Marcy" What's Good

> Holla At Ya Boy
> "The Truth"
> MikeyRaw

Chapter One

I N SEARCH OF THE LIGHT...

I've gone down for the third time, yet the pain still exists, I'm fighting with all of my might...for the people, the places, the things that I'd miss...

Consumed by darkness, I can barely see the light...

Wondering if it's over, I reflect on my life.

Did "God" love me? Did he embrace me as a child, and again as a man? Was he forgiving like I was told? Did he truly understand? I wonder if he answered my prayers?... I've had a few enemies in my life... Could this possibly be the answer to theirs?

So many things that I've taken for granted... When God blessed me with life, did I mess it up?... Or is this how He planned it? He knew my heart! My intentions were pure! God knows I didn't wanna live like this anymore!

I've lived my life with the absence of guidance and no sense of direction... I prayed for all of the above and had faith in his protection.

Was it all a nightmare?... Or simply a mixture of good and bad dreams? I've been dying from the beginning... At least that's how it seems...

Is it really over? Will I never see the light? I mean...I can see it a little, but it's just not that bright.

...Angels surround me... My breathing has ceased... I see the

light... I've finally found peace!

"Branded a Beast"

The courtroom was crowded, fortunately with people I did not know, because I tend to feel extremely uncomfortable in court no matter the circumstances and I never wanted to be seen by any family, friends, or associates in a vulnerable state and for some reason I felt that way on this day... It was my sentencing day, and even though I plead guilty and had complete knowledge of exactly what it was I was facing, I still felt unsafe.

It might have been my mind playing tricks on me, but it seemed really cold in the courtroom, to the point where I could have sworn I saw my breath. My attorney (Attore, Angelo) did the best he could and I believe that! He approached me after conversing with the prosecutor, dressed in his navy blue, three button suit, w/cuff links and initials in his sleeves and soft Italian leather shoes. He noticed my feeling of uneasiness and gave me a look that said everything would be okay. Truthfully, I appreciated his attempt but at the same time a sudden flash of anger and hurt consumed me because it was at that moment that I realized I was really alone. It was hard to accept the fact that my paid attorney seemed to be the closest thing I had to a friend *or* family in the courtroom! That fact left a bitter taste in my mouth and it was hard as hell to swallow!

"How you holding up, kid?" my attorney asked.

"I'm cool," I replied with my pride in the way knowing I wasn't ready to go to the penitentiary. I needed a little more time out there, just a few days. To do what? Only God knows, but I needed them!

That's the funny thing about *time*...it waits for no man!

My attorney was talking to me and I know I should have been listening, but they say that your life flashes before your eyes right before you die, and I don't know about dying in the sense of death, but being sent to prison to me was the equivalent of it and my life was definitely flashing before me.

I hadn't even lived yet so I definitely wasn't ready to die. I didn't care if I was only facing seven-and-a-half years! At sixteen years of age, those years seemed like forever. Damn near half of my life that I had already lived. I tried my hardest to do the mental math and I thought about what I was doing seven-and-a-half years ago at the age of eight. That didn't help matters because it was so long ago and so many things had happened in between then and now that I couldn't even remember! One thing I did remember about back then was that I wasn't on my way to prison!

We stood when the judge entered the courtroom and I noticed that it got real quiet! It amazed me every time; the respect, the power, the fear, whatever it was. I wanted it but I knew that I could never be no judge, but that power, that respect, and that fear were an attainable goal of which they had no clue at all that every moment away from society, from my life, there was a contribution on *their* part to the creation of that which would one day cause my name alone to demand and warrant all of the above! I stepped up next to my attorney at the judge's request and wondered *How could they have the audacity to make a man stand up to receive a sentence that was given to knock him down?*

"Anthony Fennel," the judge spoke in a voice that was stern and loud. "You have entered a plea of guilty to the count of murder in the third degree. Before I render my sentence, is there anything you would like to say on your behalf?"

I studied this speech time and time again, and I knew it by heart, but I began to stutter. I hated myself for that. *(Fuck these crackas, I'm me.)*

"Take your time," my attorney said to me.

"Your Honor, I know there is nothing at this point in time that can be said or done that could even begin to justify my actions, and I don't want to sound selfish or anything because I accept full responsibility for them, but truthfully, I can only accept your sentence and hope and pray for the best. I've done a great deal of thinking over the course of the last eight months and I know, Your Honor, that I am capable of doing much better with my life! I don't blame my history for my actions and I wish it would have never happened, but unfortunately, it did and I'd like to take this time to extend my sincerest and deepest apologies to the decedent's family and everybody in this courtroom for having to be here today on my behalf, but most importantly to the victim's family for their loss... Thank you."

It amazed me how my every word was clung to and here I was, a sixteen-year-old black boy in a sea of white faces, but just for that moment, if only for that one moment, I felt powerful!

"In life, where the world is plagued with problems," the judge continued, "we seem to always search for the easiest of answers, and I can assure you that there is never an answer to any problem at the hand of a gun! I listened to your words and I've given a great deal of thought to this particular case and I have come to the conclusion that you are very smart for your age. I believe there *is* light at the end of your tunnel, but I can tell you with no second thought that if you choose to continue on your path, going in the wrong direction, you will be consumed by darkness. In light of the circumstances involved in this case, I am going to go along with the plea that has been set forth.

"Anthony Fennel, you are hereby sentenced to serve a sentence of no less than seven-and-a-half years and not to exceed the maximum of fifteen years!"

I wasn't surprised, but at the same time, even knowing the outcome; to hear it in its finality sent chills through my body, but I was glad that it was finally over! All the court appearances, visits with my attorney and the wondering that consisted of a lot of *"what ifs"* was finally over!

I think about the night that led me to prison and it seems like five minutes ago even with every day that has passed...especially the events that played out beforehand! Being from *"Second Street,"* also known as *"The Deuce,"* very few things are ever expected of you other than to break the law, and do your best to survive and take advantage of any opportunity that presents itself, good or bad, but ultimately to end up in prison or to become another statistic by being shot and killed in the streets. As harsh as that reality may seem, it was the truth and very few people have lived to prove otherwise! It was never actually told to you verbally except in a heated moment by your mother or somebody else's mother, but for the most part, it was just accepted as common knowledge! Back in the day, everybody seemed to be a friend because as kids we knew that we needed each other.

"J.O." happened to be one of my closest friends during that time and I also had a homie named "X" that had been in *Juvie* for six months on a robbery charge. About eight months prior to "X" going in, I was messing with this young girl named Vanessa and she liked to tell me things about her family, like how she be seeing crazy amounts of money and drugs in her cousin's house all the time, and he never looks out for her and her mom with anything. She was hip to the fact that me and my squad were trying our best to make a name for ourselves and were hustling, as far as sticking up all the stores, *and* people on the streets, and taking all the money we made and putting it together to cop some coke off of *"Finesse,"* who, before he was killed, was the closest thing we've ever been to a real live boss! Vanessa was consistent with her stories and I only listened because I wanted some pussy, but one day I saw some truth to what she was saying. Her cousin showed up at her house one day and one thing was for certain, this cat was about his work. The big gold chains and *Slick Rick* diamond rings he wore, along with the big bankroll he pulled out of his pocket that looked like a million dollars confirmed everything that Vanessa told me about this cat.

It was all coming to me clearly now. Cuzo handed Vanessa a hundred dollar bill and asked her to go get him something to eat. I never robbed a man in his home, but "X" had done it once before with some older dudes from the hood and I decided right then and there that *this man, my girl's cousin,* would be my very first victim. If he walked around with that type of money, his home was well worth the risk. I had placed my life and freedom in jeopardy so many times before for next to nothing and this was my chance…the big break, I wanted *and* needed.

I called X that night and once I explained to him how dude was shining with the jewelry and flashing stacks of hundreds, there was nothing more to be said. It was as good as done!

We got our squad together and decided it was best to do it during the morning hours when nobody would be expecting anything to happen. We agreed on a Sunday because even a drug dealer needs a day of rest, and after a long hard weekend on the town, Sunday seemed like the right day. Even God rested on Sunday! Or so I've heard!

I spent every day with Vanessa that week hoping that

she would tell me more about her cousin, but she never did and I didn't wanna seem like I was fishing for info, so I left it alone. I knew where he lived and that was all I needed.

Everybody in my squad played a certain role. *Kwon* was a planner and a thinker. *X* was just wild with it on all levels, down for whatever. *Double-M* was quiet, but dangerous because he was an extremist. *Y.T.* was a bonafied hustler and a ladies man. He could bag bitches for everyone *and he did!* *Ani-Dog* was a soldier's soljah! He hustled but he was more infatuated with guns rather than bitches and money. *Ant-Live* was a hustler by any means and the funniest fat nigga I ever met. He could make a nigga laugh at his own funeral. *Me*, I was all of the above and I wanted more for myself which meant that I wanted more for my team as well. It was only right! I could talk my crew into and out of anything and I wouldn't hesitate to get on the front line to make things happen. They were my family.

J.O. was my homie because he was just a cool, fly ass nigga. He had been selling weed since he was 11 years old and other than that, he was just there, which was cool with me. Ani-Dog and Ant-Live were always fucking with J.O., but that was just the way they were.

Sunday arrived fast and it was time to get it in! We all met at Y.T.'s house because his mother was never there. We prepared ourselves for our *Big Break.*

We all wore sweats, black or blue, and we planned to use ski masks to shield our identity.

"Yeah, yeah, we 'bout to be some rich muthafuckin' niggaz and that's my word. If this nigga act like he wanna try a nigga, I'm leaving 'em for dead," X stated excitedly. He was dead serious about murking something so if the cousin played hard to get, X wasn't gonna hesitate to plug him.

"I hear that," Ani-Dog and Double-M answered simultaneously.

"Yo, be easy 'cause it ain't even gonna be that type of party. Would you try anything wit' seven burners in your face? Hell, no! We gonna be cool, get in and get the fuck out. He's just like a big store, and we ain't shooting nothing if we ain't got to. You feel me?" I said to get everyone on the same page.

Kwon went to steal a car and let it be known that he wanted to be present, but he would be the lookout and the driver. Everybody understood, and it was better that way. The brodie game wasn't in him so it would have been foolish to force his hand!

We pulled up to the niggaz' house in a conversion van and circled the block once to get a good look around. It wasn't even 10 o'clock in the morning yet, so we figured that most of the neighbors would probably be sleep. We parked at the end of the block and got out. Ant-Live, Ani-Dog, and J.O. went around back while the rest of us went up to the front door. I stood on the side because this nigga already saw me once before and I wasn't really trying to be noticed.

J.O. shouldn't have been there because truthfully this wasn't for him, but he wanted to get paid too. Y.T. knocked on the door bare faced and for a minute we began to think that nobody was there until a little boy around six years old answered the door in some pajamas with *Scooby Doo* all over them. He looked up at Y.T so Y.T. asked him, "Is your daddy home?"

"He's sleep with my mommy," the little boy replied. I felt bad about the whole situation but at the same time I refused to leave empty handed so it was a must that I get mines by any means necessary!

Y.T. pulled some money out of his pocket and said, "I have to give him this money. He knows I'm coming so I'ma run it up to him real quick." He just walked right past the little boy and we immediately followed suit, each one of us bare faced! Once we reached the staircase, we put on our masks and I took one look back and noticed the little boy laid out on a blanket lost in the T.V. Double-M went to the back to let the crew in and informed them to stay downstairs and keep an eye out, and that everything was cool.

At the top of the staircase, we parted separate ways and I had a 9 millimeter luger. I was real nervous even with the burner in my hand because we were in the process of violating a man's home!

I was the first one to spot the bedroom and I wasn't actually trying to be the first on the scene so I motioned to get Y.T.'s attention.

Y.T. opened the door quietly and as he did I noticed Vanessa's cousin laid on his back with the prettiest, sexiest chocolate bitch I ever seen. Even in her sleep, she was a dime as she laid across his chest with her pretty black hair covering his neck. Her breasts were partially exposed from one side and I could see her ass. It was so voluptuous and perfectly round in its fullness and she didn't have any panties on under the nightie she had that was raised up on her hips. We were young as hell and for a second, we got stuck on stupid staring at this beautiful black bitch! I eased over to the right side of the bed where the broad was and Y.T. went to the left. I shook my head and held my breath and as I took a step closer, the nigga subconsciously shifted his body and began mumbling some shit that was inaudible. I put my burner next to the bitch's head and nudged her just enough to get her attention. She didn't move so I pushed a little harder and at the same exact time, Y.T. was doing the same to the dude, only he was tapping him on his head with the barrel of a bulldog. Their eyes opened at the same time and for some reason, nobody said a word, which kind of had me fucked up because it was expected. The fact that there were no screams was good though! Y.T. kept the distance between him and dude just in case homeboy tried some heroic type shit.

"You know what it's hitting for, so you can make this shit easy or make it rough, the choice is yours, nigga," Y.T. spoke firmly but in a low tone.

"Where's my son? Please! Don't hurt my baby. Please!" the woman's voice threw me for a second because the bitch was black as night but had a Spanish accent.

I cut her off and said, "Your son is cool, but if this muthafucka right here," I pointed my gun in her man's direction, "don't come up off of what we came for, I can't promise you he'll remain that way, so what's it gonna be, muthafucka?"

"Listen, you ain't gotta hurt nobody. The money is in my pants over there." He motioned towards a wicker chair where a pair of gray slacks were draped over the back. Neither of us moved.

SMACK. Y.T. came down on the nigga's face wit' the butt of his gun. Blood flowed through Y.T.'s fingers down towards his wrist while dude's voice got real nasal.

"What do you muthafu...what do you want?" he caught himself.

"Everything! Nigga, if you make one more attempt to insult my intelligence, I'ma let this muthafucka do all the talking from here on out! You hear me?" Y.T. was wiggling his gun indicating that his heat would dictate the show from now on.

Dude shook his head in agreement.

I told the broad to get up out of the bed and as she did, dude grabbed her hand so I yanked her up by her nightie and it ripped, completely exposing her big, black, soft, but firm titties with nipples the size of a quarter that were damn near purple. My dick got hard instantly. I told the bitch to put the robe on that was on the floor. She was a bad bitch too, but a nigga didn't need them type of distractions. At least, not at this particular moment. We were playing a dangerous game!

I began to tie the bitch's wrists with the string to the robe and made her lie face down on the floor near the foot of the bed. She was sniffing and crying a prayer, I guess in Spanish.

We got the nigga up off the bed and as he got out from under the covers, I realized that I ain't have shit to offer this grown ass beautiful bitch on the floor. He was butt ass naked and I wasn't on no gay shit, but the nigga was type abnormal. Just the same, under any circumstances, I would have fucked the shit out of that bitch on the floor, but the rape game was for another type of nigga. Definitely not me!

J.O. came through the door while Y.T. was in the middle of tying dude up with some ripped sheets. I had my gun pointed directly at the nigga with his face full of blood.

"Come on, y'all! What's up? We trying to be out, man," J.O. said, sounding real scary.

"We 'bout to get what we came for now, ain't that right playa?" I said.

He shook his head and disgustedly said, "The safe, it's behind the dresser, the one over there." He was using his head to point in the direction of his stash.

Me and J.O. went over and moved the dresser easily. There was definitely a safe in the wall. My heart sped up knowing that I would find in that safe something that would make my every day that much better.

"What's the combination?" J.O. asked. Y.T. backed his question up by placing the barrel of his gun to dude's temple.

"31 left, 20 right, and 14 left," the cousin answered.

"31-20-14, hurry up, nigga," I said to J.O. as he began

to twist and turn the black and silver dial.

"Got it! Oh, shit! Yo, we up, nigga. Oooooh, we up!" J.O. spoke with all types of excitement.

In the safe were stacks of money, a scale and three bricks of coke. I had never seen a brick in my life other than on T.V., so my mind was racing with thoughts that wherever there was a brick, there was a lot of money.

I grabbed the black silk pillow case off the bed and we started throwing everything into it. J.O. spotted a chrome Mac-11 in the back of the safe hanging on two hooks. He grabbed it and we walked over towards the bitch, picked her up and we tied her and her man together and covered their mouths with sheet strands. Honestly, I felt bad! Not for them, *fuck them*, but the little boy really had no idea what was happening upstairs and I knew he would have to be the one to discover his parents tied up and his daddy bleeding. Oh well! It comes with the game! He'll be alright, 'cause I'm alright and I've witnessed a lot worse than that in my life.

Before leaving, I went over to the pants on the chair and retrieved another chunk of money and told the nigga as aggressively as I could, "This ain't got shit to do with business, nigga. It's personal. I warned you not to be out there," With that, I smacked him across his forehead so he could feel my words! I felt the need to do that because I was 6'1" and could be easily taken as a grown man. So instead of searching for a bunch of young boys, his mind would be focused on whoever he had beef with at any point in time. After violating this nigga's home, there would definitely be consequences and repercussions. I just hoped it would be directed at the wrong niggaz!

As we came down the stairwell, I looked at a clock on the wall. The same clock I glanced at on the way up and although it had seemed like forever, we had only spent seventeen-and-a-half minutes doing what we did. I also noticed the little boy asleep on his blanket, looking peaceful with the T.V. on blast. I looked at him one last time and wondered if anybody else in the room thought what I was thinking! Only God knew!

We all exited through the back yard and before we hit the main street, we got a quick look around. Everything was good so we made our way to the van.

"Listen, everybody be easy and Kwon, drive right, baby, 'cause we did the damn thing," Y.T. spoke with excitement in his voice.

I was the fastest as far as running, so I sat shotgun with the black silk pillowcase in hand. Just in case worse came to worse, I had easy access to break.

Thankfully, nothing happened and we reached Y.T.'s house safely. Kwon took the van and wiped it down and left it stranded over by Cumberland Projects. One thing for certain, it wouldn't be there in the morning!

Everybody was anxious to actually see what we came off with, but I promised Kwon I would wait till he got back and I was true to my word. Niggaz acted as if they felt some type of way about the shit, but we waited...impatiently.

Finally, Kwon came into the room. We had all hung out in Y.T.'s room before, but today seemed different. It was! Today, we sat in his little ass, dirty, cluttered room with a treasure that would effect the rest of our lives, some for the better, and others for the worse!

"Go on and empty the shit, dog. Why you being so damn dramatic?" Double-M said.

And on cue, as always, Ani-Dog said, "Yeah, why you being so dramatic?"

"Be easy yo, I got this," I said in response.

We stood in amazement as we watched all the contents fall onto the bed. Everybody started reaching out to grab money. I reached in and grabbed a brick. I was proud of myself and I knew that I would never be fucked up again. I was up!

"A yo, calm the fuck down! Put that shit back on the bed and stop acting like y'all ain't ever had shit." I couldn't believe I was hearing Ant-Live correctly. Everybody complied.

"Man, fuck you!" Kwon broke the silence in a homie type way and we all broke out laughing.

Then Live said, "Nah, for real though, we gotta count this shit all out."

After close to forty minutes, we had all the money stacked into one-thousand dollar piles. Sixty-seven stacks to be exact, including the money I had taken out of the pants. Yeah, I was far from a grimy nigga with my niggas. We broke bread evenly. Nine Gs a piece and it was agreed that me and Y.T. would get the extra four Gs to split which was only right. It may not seem like much, but to a bunch of niggaz who were teenagers and never really had shit, it seemed like each of us had hit the lottery!

J.O. wanted to keep the Mac-11, but ended up being talked out of it by Ani-Dog for 700 ones!

We had plans to sell the coke to Finesse, at a wholesale price, once we figured out exactly what that was, but after listening to Kwon, who always had a plan, we decided against it.

"Dig, that nigga Finesse ain't ever really look out for us. I say we take this shit and dub it up! No ounces, no grams, just all twenty pieces. We could make a killing, and besides the fact, we can't trust no muthafuckas out here. We all of a sudden pop up with weight for sale, it ain't gonna take but one crab ass nigga to put two and two together and make four and then we got drama we don't need. I'm telling you muthafuckas right now, don't try and brag about this shit, not even to no bitches. Especially not to no bitches."

Kwon was right and we all agreed!

Me and Y.T. spent the next week, as well as Ant-Live and J.O. breaking the work down. We got a fiend to rent us two rooms in a cheap ass motel for the week, and the smell from the coke was a nauseating smell. Wild chemicals! Sometimes our hands would begin to feel numb, so we would take turns breaking it down, free handing it, weighing the stones with our eyes!

For the next month and a half, we had the time of our lives, taking small losses here and there, but we really didn't notice or maybe we just didn't care because it was all profit no matter how you looked at it. Whoever said money don't change people was lying.

Especially for a muthafucka who ain't ever had it. Your character literally changes. You find confidence in areas you never did before. Females was shooting their shot at us trying to get in. I wasn't turning down nothing but my collar at the time! I was *that* deal!

Word was out on the street about what had happened and also that dude that we stuck had some cat out here to lay the niggaz who did it to rest. *Us.*

Evidently, we fucked up somewhere along the line 'cause we got bold, scrambling, trying to make and break a dollar thinking that the nigga would never find out. *So we thought.*

It was winter time and cold as a muthafucka, snowing like crazy! Me and my shortie at the time, Tracey, were inside her mother's house. Tracey was a broad I been trying to get at since seventh grade, who finally submitted to a power greater than hers. It was convenient that she lived right on the block 'cause I had easy access to her crib *and* a view of my hood. Dirty and crowded usually, but because of the weather and snow, it seemed peaceful and beautiful, but it was only an illusion! I sat at the windowsill and noticed a car running at the end of the block. A black Buick Regal that I had never seen before. I watched for about five minutes when a nigga with real short dreds stepped out of the back seat and dipped into the alley. When he came out a second later, he had a mask on with a gun at his side. At the same moment, I noticed J.O. walking up the block by the pay phones.

I didn't even bother to grab my coat. With a pair of jeans, a wife beater on and slippers, I grabbed my burner from under the couch and raced down the stairs, three and four steps at a time until I hit the streets. By this time, J.O. was walking right up on the cat. *How the hell he didn't see him?* Damn.

The masked man, who I would later find out to be *Kareem Daniels* A.K.A. *Shiesty,* with his gun in hand, stretched his arm out and fired once, hitting J.O. in his upper right arm. I fired three or four times as I ran across the street and hit him with the second shot, but the first and the last two missed. As the bullet entered his body, he twisted and pushed off the wall in an attempt to regain his position, but it was too late.

I always wondered what it would be like to kill a man and now was a perfect time as any. I knew it was wrong, but something inside assured me that it was right!

As he tried to raise his gun for the last time, I fired a single shot right through the mask hitting him right above his left eye!

I stood there frozen, feeling the breeze on my face and the heat from the burner in my hand. My heart raced wildly. Truthfully, I loved the way it felt...I was officially on the other side! I was a murderer!

Chapter Two
REBIRTH

I can't believe I just sat up in this nut ass halfway house for "New Year's," the Millennium. What the fuck was I thinkin' 'bout? I know it took a whole lot of restraint to sit here and watch that shit from a window and not walk up out this muthafucka. Time definitely changes things 'cause I remember a time when I wouldn't have thought twice about that shit and here I am, seven days after the fact. Tomorrow is my twenty-third birthday and I ain't had a birthday on the streets since I was fifteen, and I'm still sitting in this muthafucka...

"Anthony," the sound of the counselor's voice called out while I was deep in my own thoughts. "Anthony," I hear this bitch, but at the same time I don't, 'cause all I'm thinkin' 'bout now is how sexy this ol' ass broad is, especially since I ain't been with a woman in over six-and-a-half years.

"Mr. Fennell," she said loud enough to bring me back!

"Yeah, what's up?" I responded.

"What's up? We don't answer people around here with *what's up* and secondly, you haven't heard a word I've been saying to you. Now, if you don't wanna be here, that's fine with me and you always have the option to say so, but you know the consequences of that and if..." I cut her short.

"Diane, why is it that every time we sit in this office you feel the need to remind me of the fact that I can go back to prison? I know that. You think I don't? I just got caught up in my thoughts, that's all. Damn."

She offered me a soft semi-smile and said, "You're right, so, how about this, a penny for your thoughts."

Bitch, you getting on my nerves and this counseling shit is for a nigga named "not me" and if we ain't fuckin', let it be known 'cause you teasing the shit outta me! Of course, I couldn't say that, so I played along and replied, "A penny? All that good money the government gives you and you only offering a penny? So my thoughts must not be worth much, huh?" I hit her with the ill smirk.

There goes that full smile! Damn, I'm sharp. This bitch could have me under different circumstances.

"You know what I mean," she replied.

"Yeah, I know what you mean, but I just have some things on my mind right now and truthfully, talking 'bout it ain't gonna change the situation."

"Well, you never know, so if you feel like talking tomorrow, just put a request slip in my mail slot, alright?" Diane concluded cordially.

"Alright," I ended.

Damn, that broad need to give a nigga some type of rhythm for real. We could be spending that hour doing a whole lot more important things than talking about a nigga's past. If I was free, I probably wouldn't even pay her ol' ass no mind. She's too tall, too blonde, too white, and to top off that, she ain't workin' with no ass at all! She got that disease, *Noasatol*. She be saying a lot of shit that makes sense though, but just not to me because I got my mind set on some money. Not a funky ass paycheck either! *Big things*.

* * * * * * * *

"A yo' Ant, what up?"

"Ain't shit. What's good, Big-Dee, where you coming from?"

I really didn't care, but Big-Dee, who was the littlest nigga I ever met, was one of the very few people I accepted as worthy of being associated with given the circumstances, so I spoke to speak. Besides, he was entertaining like a muthafucka. Funny as hell!

He responded. "I just had a one-on-one with my counselor 'cause you know a nigga trying to raise up real soon." He said that like he felt the need to justify his being obedient. "Anyway, fuck all that. Did you hear about ya man Boom?" he asked. Big-Dee was always getting all the gossip and figured that this was some more shit to share.

When I got to this place, my man Boom was already here for like three-and-a-half months, but he decided that it was three-and-a-half months too long and set himself free about two weeks ago, by way of escape!

"No, I ain't heard nothing 'bout that nigga, but what's up? You hear anything?" I replied.

"Yeah, that nigga free," Big-Dee announced.

"Yeah, I'm hip, but what else?" I was trying to find if anything else popped off.

"No, I mean he's free for real. When he bounced, he called his parole officer and told him that he messed up and that he got stressed out and what not, and dude told him that if he found a job within a week that he wouldn't violate him, so now that nigga is working up in his brother's barber shop, free as a muthafucka."

"A yo, Dee, say that's your word." I was bugging because I never thought that these crackers would give a nigga a break for doing some stupid shit like that.

"That's my word."

"Who put you on?" I was still tripping off the info so I wanted to see if it was a rumor or if it was facts.

"I just heard the counselors talking about that shit when I was coming out the office, but yo, I'ma holla at you later after I go to group, aiight?"

"Yeah, yeah, do that."

The nigga Boom got away with the shit. Knowing my luck, it wouldn't even go down that way because if it wasn't for bad luck, I wouldn't have any luck at all! This shit ain't for me though, so I might just try my hand, and if I blow, what's eighteen months or two years compared to the six-and-a-half years I just put in? Fuck it, I'ma go ahead and do me, but I'ma wait till after 6 o'clock so my P.O. don't get wind of my early release until tomorrow at least. I gotta try and get upstairs to call my shorty. As a matter of fact, I ain't gonna hip her to this shit because she ain't gonna do nothing but try and talk me out of it! I got a birthday to celebrate and I'ma celebrate it until they catch me! Happy birthday, nigga.

* * * * * * *

"Evelyn, let me holla at you for a minute." Evelyn was a monitor at the place and she had been on my team since I got there, letting me touch all on her here and there, but she wasn't doing any fuckin' at all. I talked to her a few times about leaving, but I think I just wanted to hear her talk me out of it, which she always seemed to do, but this time, it wasn't gonna be none of that. No sir, because tonight, I'm taking flight!

In her soft, sexy ass Spanish accent, she said, "Hey, Poppi, que' pasa?"

Quickly I said, "I just wanted to let you know that I'm gonna see you real soon on the other side." I smiled at her.

"What's that supposed to mean?" she questioned while squinching and contorting her brow.

"It means, I'm out tonight and I mean it this time. I'm also trying to maintain some type of contact wit' you."

"Why you be talking crazy all the time? What happened this time?" she said, looking around as if to see if anyone else could hear us.

I poked at the center of her chest without actually touching her and said, "Time happened, but I'm telling *you* because I know you ain't gonna cross me up, and like I said, I'm trying to see you, Ma!" I smiled at her again and could tell by her hesitation that either my words or my charming smile had her right where I wanted her.

"So what are you gonna do? And where are you gonna go? You should wait until tomorrow to see if you feel the same because you know what's gonna happen, don't you?" she said with sincerity in her eyes.

"Yeah, I'm hip to the consequences and right now, Ma, the end is justifying the means, and as far as everything else, I'm built for them streets. The question is, are those streets built for me?"

She said, "Hold on. Let me write my number down for you. Do you need a couple of dollars? Damn, Papi, I don't believe I'm sitting here condoning this shit, but you gotta be your own man, just be safe 'cause things ain't the same out there." She was writing her number down for me.

I wanted to accept the offer for the ones that she offered since I was on that "E" like crazy, but after the fly shit I just popped to her, to accept some ends would be like contradicting my confidence and my ability to get right! So, I got her number and promised to call and said, "I'm good with the money. Just do me a favor and make sure Big-Dee keeps cigarettes and shit, aiight?" With that said, I went back upstairs and ran everything down to Big-Dee while I packed my shit and changed my clothes. He wasn't feeling the shit at all, but what could he do but tell me to be safe and as always in parting, said, "Yo, Ant, hold ya head, kid."

As I walked out the door, I stopped and looked at my lil homie and said, "Finish this shit and if I'm there when you touch down, you gon' do some eating with me, and as far as holding my head, I'ma most definitely do that 'cause one thing's for certain, ain't nobody gonna do it for me." With that I winked at him and got to beating my feet.

I can't lie, the walk downstairs to the first floor and front door seemed like it took forever, like if I was drifting in a Spike Lee movie, just taking it all in, but I made it and when I did, it seemed like nobody even noticed me except for Evelyn who was sitting at a table right by the door not wanting to look up at me. I touched her shoulder and said, "I've never been more ready."

With my bag on my shoulder, I kicked the front door open with all my might, which wasn't really necessary, but I wanted the added dramatic effect. The alarm went off, louder and more clear than I've ever heard it before. I regretted it the instant that the alarm went off, but there was no turning back, even if I wanted to, so I held my head up high and entered the cold jungle with absolutely no destination in mind! I had no idea of where I was going, but I was determined to get there!

I walked for about five minutes, until I ended up at an apartment complex that I semi-grew up in and used an old trick I once used as a kid in order to get into the buildings when I was out too late and knew that my mother wasn't gonna press the buzzer to let me up. I pressed all of the buttons for all of the apartments and said, "It's me," until somebody decided to buzz me up, probably thinking they knew the person on the other end of the speaker. When the door buzzed, I pulled it open and sat there on the steps by the radiator to get some heat, and to see if anyone would come out of their apartments. Finally, after about five minutes of waiting and absorbing the heat, I found a spot for my bag, which was too heavy to be carrying around, especially with no place to really go...at least not close by...and left it there with hopes that nobody would find it and take it.

I stepped back outside and walked down to *The V*, a park where kids, who once upon a time had dreams to be a variety of different things and still had the potential to make them a reality, myself included, slowly, but surely cashed in on their dreams for a lifestyle that seemed so promising...this lifestyle we call *The Game*. Who would have known.

As I sat there by the basketball courts, I went down memory lane and smoked my first fresh *Newport* as a free man and thought to myself, *Damn, it really don't taste any different.*

A few minutes went by and I noticed a figure coming towards the basketball court. I doubted that it would be anybody I knew, especially since nobody really hung around there anymore and all my homies who were considered friends at the time, split up for one reason or another and took claim to other parks and other blocks throughout the city. As the figure got closer, I noticed it was a young boy, about seventeen or eighteen years old, approaching me with a blunt in his hands. As he licked the edges to make the final preparations for what I like to call *A trip to that place*, because a blunt that size would definitely take you there, he asked me if I had some *fire* on me. *I know this kid!* It was my man Junior's lil nephew, Bobby, only he wasn't little any more and he damn sure didn't seem to possess that innocence he once did.

When I passed him a lighter, he realized who I was and said, "Ant, you don't remember me, fam?"

"Yeah, I remember you. What's good with you?" I said, extending my hand for a salutation.

"I ain't seen you in a long time. You know my uncle Junior got twenty to forty years on a body. That nigga was out here losing his mind fuckin' wit' that leak."

"Yeah, I heard about that shit. Next time you holla at him, let him know that I touched down and asked about him."

He hesitated for a minute and said, "I heard you had gotten forty years and the nigga J.O. had sold you out and ain't get no time. What's really good wit' that?"

I smiled and said, "Last thing I heard, I had life on two bodies, so you know how that shit goes. Muthafuckas' just wanna rap 'cause they was blessed with a hole in they face. The nigga J.O. ain't get any time because he ain't do nothing! I got seven-and-a-half to fifteen years and I ended up doing six-and-a-half on that."

He held out the blunt that he hadn't even lit yet and said, "Welcome home, my nigga. If you ain't on paper, go ahead and make it official."

I grabbed it and he held the lighter out to me.

While we sat there and smoked, I asked, "A yo, Bobby, dig this here. What happened to you wanting to go to school to play ball for Syracuse?"

He shocked me with his response, but at the same time he didn't. He said, "No disrespect, my nigga, but muthafuckas don't call me Bobby any more..."

I guess I ain't have to ask why, as he continued.

"...and as far as playing ball, I got two bullets lodged in my leg and that shit wasn't nothing but a dream anyway 'cause you know how this shit go out here. Them white folks painted the park and changed some shit to look all nice and shit, but when a cat try to cover up, they shit in the litter box. When it all comes down to it, it's still shit up under that litter, you feel me?"

"Yeah, I feel you, my nigga, I definitely feel you on that!

You still staying with your auntie? Let me use the phone."

He reached into his jacket and handed me a cell phone. I was a little embarrassed 'cause I ain't know how to use it because the last time I was on the street, a cell phone was as big as a brick and came with a back pack. I toyed with it, but ain't nothing happen and *Bobby*, I mean *Smoke*, saw what was going down and said, "Just dial the area code, number and press send, the button on the right." He pointed.

I did just that and I dialed my sister's number. She picked up on the fourth ring, sounding irritated. I wondered if she knew already.

"Ebony, I need you to come scoop me up."

She must not have recognized my voice because she answered, "Who is this?"

I said, "It's your brother, who the hell you think it is? I need you to come get me."

She relaxed her voice and said, "Where you at? Hold up, what you mean come get you? Wait a minute, I know you ain't play yourself and do what I think you did."

I can imagine how she looked on the other end of the phone, hand on her hip, neck wiggling like a break dancer and her chewing some gum like if someone put a whole pack of *Doublemint* in a hungry pit bull's mouth.

"Listen, I ain't got time for all that right now. I'll rap to you when I get there, just come get me at the V."

She told me she didn't have her car, but to catch a cab and she would pay for it. That's what I did. Smoke chilled with me until the cab came, and as always in parting, he said, "Yo, hold ya head, things ain't the same out here." Why did I believe him?

I told the cab driver to pull around on 6th Street and I scooped up my bag and we drove for what seemed to be an eternity. I looked out of the window and took in the scenery which might not have been much to look at, but to me, I waited six-and-a-half years for this moment and I don't think I'd ever seen anything more beautiful. Then again, it could have been that good green that was consuming my mind at the time. Who knows!

When the cab was paid for, I stepped inside my little sister's one-bedroom apartment and the first thought that popped into my mind was *This shit ain't gonna cut it*. My sister didn't say anything to me—she just handed me the phone. I grabbed it, looked at her and said, "Yo, who this?" and a real familiar voice came from the other side of the line. It was my man J.O., the same J.O. that I took all that time for to protect, and the very same J.O. who ain't looked out for me for the past six-and-a-half years. I felt some type of way about it, but I was too high to be upset, so I said, with all sincerity as my little sister stood there listening, "I fucked up."

Without any hesitation, he responded, "Nah, nigga, you ain't fuck up. You did what half these niggaz out here did. Now you just gotta do what's best for you. I'm coming through there in about fifteen minutes unless you wanna walk up to the bar."

I wasn't about to walk outside, because the weed had me paranoid and I felt like I was on *Amerikas Most Wanted*, so I told him to just come through and to be by himself, not to let anyone know that I was here!

"I'll be there in a minute. Holla at ya sis and hold tight. Oh, yeah, welcome home, my nigga!"

As soon as I hung the phone up, my sister started asking me what happened, why I did it and what am I gonna do. She even told me to turn myself in and maybe the parole people would be easy on me. I couldn't really explain it to her because she couldn't *or* wouldn't understand if I did, so I said, "Everything is gonna be alright. And if you're worrying about me wanting to stay here, you don't have to worry because I know that when they come, this will probably be the first place they'll look, so be easy and let me make a few phone calls real quick," I said with more irritation than anger!

I called my shorty and told her what happened and as much as she tried to act like she was mad, I knew deep down inside she was happy as hell. This would be our first time seeing each other outside of prison *or* the halfway house visiting so I knew her anger was nothing more than nervousness.

For the past two years since I introduced myself to her through the mail, I was a safety net for her because no matter what went wrong in her life, out in the real world, I would always play my position and console her and make her feel better. But now, here I was in the flesh, her dream come to life, and I knew she feared that things would change between us and that our dream would become a realistic nightmare. Even then, I wouldn't have known that her foresight was 20/20.

There was a knock on the back door and I ran by a window and opened it a little and told my sister to answer it. She seemed more afraid than me, as if she was the one on her way to prison.

"Who is it?" she asked, nervous as hell. Silence. "Who is it?" she repeated.

"J.O. Open the door, it's cold as hell out here."

With a sigh of relief from both myself and my sister, she slowly and cautiously opened the door.

There was a moment of uneasiness as J.O. came into the living room. He decided to break the ice as he said, "Shit, *I* need to go to the pen for a minute. Looks like they be feeding a nigga real good 'cause it's a struggle for a muthafucka to do some eating out this bitch. I see you got ya weight up." He looked me up and down and smiled at how well I had constructed my body with all that bench pressing and curling.

I wanted to say, *Fuck you, nigga, that shit ain't funny and if I ain't have as much common sense as I do, I'd pop your fuckin' top*, but now wasn't the time and I felt at that moment that I needed the nigga, so I smiled and said, "You don't wanna do that, believe me, you don't wanna do that because that shit ain't even for the birds.

"So what's the plan, kid?" he asked feeling my mood. Niggas know how to change the subject when they feel it's a little tension in the air about their current topic.

"I don't know, to be truthful. Right now I just need a place to stay until I can get my mind right. I don't want them people running all up in here finding what they looking for, feel me?"

"Yeah, I got you on that. Dig this here, my spot ain't no better because you know how I be living, so I'ma put you up in a telly for a few days until we can come up wit' a better plan, alright?"

I nodded my head in agreement and grabbed my bag as I followed the nigga out to his car. I walked behind him, hating him secretly for having the past six-and-a-half years of free air! For having all them diamonds in his shine, for having left me for dead in prison, for having his own place, his own whip and his own little cell phone that hung from his hip, but most of all, I hated the nigga for acting as though nothing ever happened between us and that everything was cool!

We got into his truck, a '99 Lincoln Navigator, cocaine white, with light tan tint on all the windows, and 22-inch rims, with peanut butter interior. I said, "If this is starving, I can't wait to do some eating."

He smiled and said, "It's hard out here for real. Don't let this bullshit fool you because it's a lot easier said than done. But I know if anybody can do it, you're just the nigga to get it done. I took a L' about four months ago up in New York trying to step my game up and it ain't been the same since. It's like overnight, the game changed. You'll see for yourself soon enough. Shit ain't the same, but fuck all that right now. I've been waiting for you and I'm glad you're home." Then he put the truck in *drive* and put the pedal to the metal.

My only response was, "Yeah, me too."

We drove around the city for about an hour, smokin' weed, talking and basically reminiscing, while we listened to a whole bunch of different CDs that I definitely wasn't hip to. As I listened to both him and the music, I saw that a lot *had* changed, and I thought about how everybody used to always tell me on the phone how I wasn't missing anything out here. They must have been crazy because even the music was more serious. Life went on without me. Who would have guessed it! Definitely not me!

He asked me if I wanted to go see anybody and I told him NO, so we headed out to the telly. He paid for the room for four days, under *his* name, gave me two hundred ones and said he'd be back the following day and if I needed anything to just holla and he'd make it happen.

Here I was, alone in a room, that felt like an apartment compared to the cells I'd been in, and I wanted to get out because I felt alone, like it was all a dream and tomorrow I'd wake up and be in the halfway house or worse, prison. So I wanted to get out and tell the world that I was home and just make the best of it in case it turned out to be a dream! I wanted to enjoy it while I could!

Instead, I called my shorty and told her to bring me a cheese steak, some pizza and some weed. So much for letting the world in on my welcome home party! I'd have to settle for some food, some smoke and some ass. I wasn't complaining! Not at all.

I took a shower and laid down on the bed as naked as the day I entered this world, waiting for Victoria to arrive. By the time she got here, I was half sleep from the trees I blew earlier, but when I saw her pretty face through the peep-hole, I became alive in more ways than one! Before I opened the door, I grabbed a towel and put it around my waist and headed back to the door.

I opened the door and she greeted me with a smile and a *"Boy!...Hmmm, you know you're wrong,"* as she walked through the door. I smelled her perfume. The scent made me lick my lips and bite the bottom one. Victoria was a woman who looked like God took the extra time to create.

At 5'6" tall, her weight was spread perfectly, and anyone who didn't know her, would assume that she worked out faithfully or danced. Her thighs were thick and firm, and that ass...damn! That ass!!! She had the type of ass that made you wanna clap and whistle out of appreciation alone. When she turned around...I looked into her hazel eyes, which gave her an air of innocence, like she was a *Church Girl*, but when I looked at her lips, those pretty red lips, with just a touch of pink and the perfect amount of clear lip gloss to give them that sexy look, and when she smiled with those lips, the freak in her manifested itself. She turned around and smiled as she placed down the bag with the food in it.

"Boy, you crazy," she said again.

All I could do was laugh. She stared at me as she shook her head and looked at me from head to toe, from toe to head, and said, "UMMM," and bit her bottom lip.

I looked back and licked my lips and said, "UMMM Yaself."

As the tug-o-war continued with our eyes caressing each other's, she came over to me and gave me a hug. Her arms wrapped around my neck. My arms wrapped around her waist and my hands pressed up against her ass.

She whispered in my ear, "I missed you, baby, and I love you."

As I turned to her, our lips met. Her lips felt like they melted in my mouth. Instantly, my dick rose to the occasion pressing firmly against the towel causing it to ease itself off of my waist to the floor. I took one of her hands from around my neck and guided it towards my dick. She let out a *"sss"* and a *"damn,"* as she began to massage me. She said, "I see you missed me too!"

I said, "More than you know, baby," and kissed her again.

As I kissed her, I backed her up to the bed and eased her down onto it. As she crawled backwards, she kicked off her shoes and I felt her breathing increase. I began to undress her and she watched me as I did, from my face to my dick, she knew that I was about to do some damage!

When her shirt came off, she reached behind herself and unsnapped her bra, and I began to work on her sweats, tugging at them, enjoying every bit of flesh as I uncovered her. Her caramel complexion was glowing like it was made in a factory...flawless. I took her socks off to reveal the prettiest feet known to man. Her toes were matching her freshly manicured nails with clear pink. She arched her back so her ass was off the bed allowing me access to pull her panties down. They were the same color as her bra, black see through lace. Once I got them off and laid my eyes on her neatly trimmed pussy, I began to think to myself like, *Damn, leaving that halfway house was definitely worth it for this.*

She looked at me while I stared at her. I began to kiss her slowly and softly on her neck, working my way down to her nipples. I eased my hand in between her thighs, teasing her spot that had become extremely wet from the feel of my fingers. She smiled at me and lifted her legs in the air, grabbing her ankles, so that her legs formed a beautiful, perfect

V shape. I could see the wetness on her folds. It seemed as if a lake or a river was beyond her pussy lips. I couldn't help but to stroke myself, wanting to dive right in without a life preserver on hoping to drown inside of her. I placed my hand between her legs to taste her juices, to taste the sweet nectar that I've craved and longed for. I began to lick the folds of her pussy and she moaned. Her hips began to move with the sensation she was feeling. She placed her legs down on the bed with her knees in an upright position towards the ceiling as I continued to lick and suck and slowly push one, two and sometimes three fingers deep inside of her, at a time! I did this for a while, to the point where *I* couldn't even take it anymore. Once I got ready to get on top of her, to move forward through her floodgates, she grabbed my arm and with her sexy, seductive smile, said, "Come here," with her finger easing towards her mouth.

I did as I was told because I aim to please...and as I obeyed her command, she reached out to my dick and began swirling her tongue around the head slowly, licking, sucking, nibbling as she played with my balls with her free hand. I began grinding teeth releasing sounds of pure pleasure. "Sss" and "damn, baby," as she tried to engulf me into her mouth. Up and down as she stroked the remainder of what wouldn't fit in her mouth while she continued to suck on me. I told her to stop before I came, and she complied with a smile. I told her that I wanted her from the back first, so I eased her off of the bed so her feet were on the floor and her hands were on the bed. As I enjoyed the view of the back of her ass, I spread her cheeks and entered her. My head flew back from the warmth and the tightness of her pussy.

"Damn, girl, this pussy feels so good." I repeated it as I pushed every inch of my manhood into her.

With a squeal of pain and pleasure, she said, "Yeah, baby...pu...push it in. Oh, shit! That's right, take it, Daddy, it's yours."

I spread her ass cheeks wider to see where I vanished to and she moaned more and more as I pulled half of my dick out of her and pushed it back in, Then I put one leg up on the bed and began to really work it.

I could feel my balls slapping against her every time I thrust deep inside of her making her scream, "Yeah, baby, ohh!...Baby...Ohh! Baby, fuck me, that's right...fuck me!!!"

I grabbed her hips and moved her so there was nothing but the floor in front of her. I placed my hand on the small of her back and told her to put her hands on the floor. Once she did that, I eased down and pushed all ten inches inside of her.

I began to pump in and out, harder, as I placed my thumb over her asshole and applied a little pressure. She shouted out, "Oh! Fuck!...Damn, boo, what are you trying to do to me...oooh!"

As I moved my thumb in a circular motion and applied more pressure, she continued to scream out, "Baby, Baby! You're making me cum. Fuck me!"

I threw her on the bed, opened her legs, set her ankles across my shoulders and entered her with a strong thrust. I told her to look at me. I said, "Cum for me, Baby...let yourself go, Baby...oh, shit, I'm cumming with you, damn! I'm cumming with you," and as we exploded, nothing in the world, at that moment seemed to be relevant, and I got lost inside of her as she did me!

We lay side by side for a while talking, smoking and truly enjoying the night, because neither of us knew what tomorrow would bring! She showered, dressed and left at 6:30 in the morning to go to work, but before she did, she turned towards me and said, "I may not fully agree with what you went through to make this all a reality, but I love you and I'm on your side, so later on, I'm gonna find us an apartment, somewhere in the cut, because now that I have you, God knows, I can't afford to lose you!" And with that, she was gone, and I fell asleep!

Chapter Three
Happy Born Day

I replayed the scenes of the night before in my dreams, over and over again, to the point where I believed that it had to be exactly that...a beautiful dream, but a dream just the same.

As I opened my eyes and saw the big ass birthday card taped to the television that hung from the wall, I knew it had to be real, and truthfully, I was unsure at that point as to how I felt about that! I got up and grabbed the card, and when I opened it, a smile consumed me as I read: *"Happy birthday, Baby! Last night was only the beginning of what has no end...My love for you. Always, V."* I knew right then how I felt about that dream that was real. I was in it to win it! No doubt about it!

I called my sister and told her I was good and that I'd see her soon. Afterwards, I took a shower and called J.O. He said he was coming to scoop me at about 7 o'clock that morning and to stay there because he had something for me. I did exactly that, thinking he was probably gonna come through with some females and a light party in mind to celebrate my birthday! I wasn't pressed, but I'd go with the flow of things.

At 7:15, I heard a light tapping at the door, and when I looked through the peephole, I saw J.O. and an old friend of mine. It was my man X. *My man.* I opened the door and said, "Yo, what's up with the secret squirrel shit?"

He responded, "What you talking about?"

"All that light tapping on the door shit."

"Nigga, you N.O.R.E.! (Nigga on the run, eating) and I know damn well you ain't trying to hear no heavy ass police knocks on the door."

"You right about that," I said, "so what's the deal? I see you woke up the dead and brought my muthafuckin' man X wit' you, so what's really good?"

X said, "Dig this here. The nigga J.O. told me it was your birthday and according to what I heard about your release from the beast, you got two things to celebrate," he said this as he lowered a back pack from his back and threw three burners on the bed, two 9 millimeter handguns and a .380, which was considered a *baby 9*! He continued, "Pick one because the choice is yours, my nigga, and a nigga can't celebrate for free."

I looked at them with questioning eyes and said, "What type of celebrating are you niggaz trying to do, 'cause I was thinking more along the lines of some bitches, some weed and a club outta town somewhere?"

J.O. said, "Yeah, that's a must, but so is opportunity and opportunity looks like an old ass Dominican nigga on the south side getting it down something major wit' all that paper stashed in his crib waiting to be took."

I asked, "How much paper?"

"Enough to celebrate and a lot more," X answered.

"So what's up, nigga? You ready to do some eating?"

I don't know exactly what happened, but I found myself

in the backseat of an old ass Honda Prelude, dressed in black sweats with a 9 millimeter handgun placed on my lap. Thoughts of going back to prison with a thousand years consumed me while *Biggie Smalls* yelled *Gimme the loot, gimme the loot* through the sound system. I felt like the kid *C* in the movie *A Bronx Tale* when he was in the car wit' his homies on the way to put some work in, all the while thinking he really didn't wanna be there. But this wasn't a movie and I ain't have a *Sonny* to save me from whatever was to come, so I was in it! I tried to convince myself that this shit wasn't about nothing. *Shit, before I got locked up, this was my thing and I was just nervous because it's been a while. Besides, what the fuck am I gonna do out here? Work under the table? Imagine that.*

Conversation was slim to none as we made our way to the south side to take advantage of *opportunity*. When we arrived, it seemed that *opportunity* lived in a big apartment complex. Not a project or a lower income complex, but an upper middle class type of complex.

I was the first to speak out of curiosity. "Which one does he live in?"

We sat and waited for about forty minutes with the lights out when X jumped up and grabbed his gun and said, "Yo, that's that muthafucka right there."

As we looked, a navy blue J-30 was pulling into the parking lot. We waited, and when he parked the car, a short Dominican with a viciously receding hairline got out of the car along with a pretty Spanish female who was cradling a bag in her chest. When they got inside, we saw a light from the apartment go on, then another. It was time to move out!

We exited the car one by one, and proceeded towards the building as if we belonged there. When we got inside the doors to the front, X said in a real soft, quiet tone, *"217, that's the one right there, 217."* He reached into his pocket and pulled out a small jar of Vaseline and with his back to the wall, reached over and smeared the Vaseline, with the tip of his finger over the peephole to apartment #217. He backed away, pulled his mask down over his face and pulled his gun from his waistline while me and J.O. followed suit.

X told me to knock on the door, lightly, and ask for something. I did exactly that and after a few knocks, a voice came to the other side of the door.

"Who is it?" with a deep, strong Spanish accent!

I replied, "It's your neighbor, Papi, 220, across the hall. I can't get in. Can I use your phone to call my wife 'cause she's sleeping?"

Silence, and then he said, "Hold on a minute."

My leg began to shake and I used the weight of the *nine* in my right hand to steady it because I was sure he was going to get a gun.

All of a sudden, I heard J.O. say, "There he go right there."

As I looked toward the front door that we came through, I saw the same Dominican cat that got out of the car staring in at us. X gave chase.

I did the same! At the front of the building, X stopped and raised his gun and attempted to let off a shot, but luckily, .380s have been known to jam up and as it did, I pushed his arm down and gave chase to the fleeing *opportunity*.

Just coming home from prison, I was in the best shape of my life, so I gave chase and caught up to him just as he was about to hit the main street and tackled him to the cold hard grass. I placed my gun to his mouth and dared him to act like he ain't understand English, 'cause a gun in the mouth is basically a universal language.

"Walk, muthafucka, and don't make a sound or you dying right here," I told him, completely in character at this point.

He said, "What you want with me, Papi?"

I said in my coldest voice, "Walk, muthafucka, or your life is what I'm taking."

He must have understood because together, we walked back towards the apartment, with the night protecting us from looking suspicious! I walked him through the front door of the apartment building and J.O. quickly grabbed him and started hitting him in the head with the butt of his gun demanding, "Where's the fucking keys? Open the door, muthafucka!"

I stopped him, to remind him that he came from the side or somewhere, so I gripped him up by his collar and told him to lead the way. He led me to the side patio door, where there were two clear sliding glass doors. As we approached them, a woman, the same woman who got out of the car, was on the other side of the glass talking on the telephone. I quickly erased the thought of her talking to the cops from my mind because she was too calm, smiling on the phone. I was five feet away from her with my gun tucked under her man's chin staring right at her and she couldn't see me because of the darkness outside. As I approached the sliding glass doors and opened them, she saw exactly what it was hitting for. Before she could scream for any type of help, X was on top of her pointing his gun at her head with his finger pressed against his lips, telling her to be quiet. He hung up the phone and handed the broad over to J.O.

We led *opportunity* to the bedroom and commenced to beating the shit out of him demanding the money *and* the work. As he balled into a fetal position to protect himself, he held his hand up as if to say *I submit* and pointed towards the dresser. I ran to the dresser and X held his face towards me for direction. On top of the dresser were about six diamond rings and some real heavy gold chains and medallions neatly arranged on a white cloth. I grabbed them and jammed them into my pocket and continued to pull the drawers out one by one until *opportunity* spoke up and said, "That one right there."

I pulled the drawer out and placed it on the bed, and as I emptied its contents onto the bed, my eyes grew wide. There were seven fat round wads of bills with rubber bands wrapped around them and a blue night bag that contained what seemed to be about a brick of coke all bagged up ready for distribution. I grabbed the bag and threw the money inside, and as I was about to call it a day, X hit him again along the side of his face and I couldn't understand it. I looked at him to tell him so, when he snapped.

"Muthafucka, you gave in too easy! Where the fuck is the work at, muthafucka? You got five seconds to say so," He cocked his gun back and continued, "or you and that pretty bitch die tonight. One, two," as he counted, I prayed, or hoped that he wasn't about to kill this man, especially when we came up. "Three, fou..."

He was cut off as *opportunity* yelled out in a hushed tone. "The closet, the closet, it's in the closet in the yellow coat. Please! Don't kill me, take it, take it all."

X was on point and I was feeling that! He dragged dude to the closet, reached up and grabbed the yellow coat that had a drawstring at the bottom of it. While this was happening, I noticed J.O. was in the room with us at the closet. I ran into the living room to see what happened with the Spanish girl. As I looked into the living room, fear took control of my mind. I saw an empty bright room with two slide doors wide open and I knew she had gone for the police! I ran back inside and said, "Yo, let's get up outta there quick, fast and in a hurry!"

As we got to the car, we left the lights out and drove for about a block before we put them on and my heart was racing faster than ever before in my life. X looked back and said, "Yo, what the fuck happened back there?"

I told him, "Yo, the bitch wasn't in the living room so she probably went for help."

J.O. just laughed and said, "I tied that bitch up. She's in the closet man. Be easy, we cool. Drive safe nigga and go to the spot."

When we got down to *the spot*, which was a building with no tenants, we poured everything onto the floor, and with the street light shining through, we examined everything. Inside of the yellow coat was an engagement ring still in the box that had about 44 ½? carats and I said, "Looks like ain't nobody getting engaged today."

Everybody laughed and J.O. said, "I know that's right, yo, that shit was sweet."

The laughing stopped as X opened the yellow jacket and nothing seemed to come out. He knew it had to be something because the coat was too heavy, so he turned it inside out and realized why nothing came out. Both sleeves and the back end of the jacket were lined with dope. Heroin. Personally I didn't know much about dope so I wasn't amazed when 2100 grams fell to the floor as the coat was ripped to shreds in search of more. My mind was on the even rolls of money facing me. I grabbed the rubber bands off and we sat for two hours counting and recounting what turned out to be $140,000!

"That's what the fuck I'm talking 'bout right there! That muthafucka was holding. He needed his shit took 'cause ain't no way in the world I'ma be getting it like that and have all that dirt where I lay my head at. Fuck that! Niggaz fuckin' crazy!" I continued, "Better him than me."

We divided the money, where each of us received $45,000. a piece! Instead of dividing the last 5 Gs, they offered it as a birthday gift. I knew better but I accepted it just the same. We put all the drugs back into the blue bag and decided that we would go to J.O.'s apartment and put everything together.

As we sat at the kitchen table, I told them, "I don't see how niggaz is starving out here and its sweet like this shit here.

X said, "Ant, I've been on the run from the same halfway house for close to nineteen months now and I ain't even had a close call yet dealing with the police. Shit seem real sweet, but believe me, it ain't. Muthafuckas ain't the same and as soon as you seem to pose a threat to another nigga's hustle, it ain't the police you have to worry about, it's the niggas, all them *in the way ass niggaz* who ain't got the fuckin' heart to get ahead. Them niggas all got 911 on speed-dial and that's the truth. Niggas will let you do some eating, but as soon as you decide to come back for seconds and thirds, guess who's coming to dinner? *One Time* will be at your door and it ain't even a joke."

From the way he spoke, I guessed he took offense to what I said, but that was only his conscience fuckin' with him. I couldn't help but to respond after J.O. put his two cents in to sign that check. I said, "I dig what you saying and all that, but on some real shit, that telling shit, it ain't nothing new and any nigga surprised by it is a fool! Muthafuckas is just more open with that shit, like it's a new fashion or something. All that's a part of the game now, 'cause muthafuckas sat back and watched it become a part of the game! I know if niggaz wasn't having burners just for the sake of having them, and a lot of these niggaz started getting their shit pushed back, making the news, all that other shit would be damn near non-existent and a whole lot of these jokers wouldn't be so eager to try and get down! You feel me?"

J.O. cut in while still separating all the work, and not looking at no one in particular, he said, "Dig right, Ant, what you trying to do about this work? I mean, I know you can make something happen wit' this coke, but that dope game is a whole nother thing. I know you ain't trying to put yourself out there and wit' this shit, you gon' have to 'cause its sweet, but at the same time, real hectic. *Real hectic!"*

"What you mean by *real hectic?"* I asked, already knowing the answer because that dope bring out the worse in a muthafucka and it's a whole different caliber of friends out there.

He said, "You ain't been home two days and you sitting on more than half of what these niggaz seen in two years, and it ain't gonna sit right wit' a lot of cats and personally, I ain't trying to see you take that trip no sooner than necessary, so why don't you take this coke, all of it and me and X will split this dope up and you keep the shines too!"

I looked up at X and he shrugged his shoulders as if to say, *It's up to you.* I didn't know much about the dope game, this much was true, but I wasn't no fucking idiot either. I knew that dope was worth a lot more than coke, and even though I knew the nigga was trying to play on my intelligence, it's more than I expected to have so it was all profit, so I agreed, but not before making a mental note: *that it was now two strikes against him! There wouldn't be a third!*

We blew an L' together to make the moment official and I used the phone to call Victoria, because I knew she was worried about not hearing from me. I was right, but I set her mind at ease and told her to meet me on 15th Street, by the pizza shop in twenty minutes. She was on her way!

I came back into the kitchen and told them I was about to smash out and get ready to do some celebrating and I would get up wit' them later on.

As I walked toward the door, with the blue bag in hand, X called my name. "Be safe, my nigga, and on some real shit, I been out here nineteen months almost for one reason and that's because a nigga put me on wit' some good advice and I followed it."

"Oh yeah? What was that?" I asked.

He said, "Niggas told me wasn't nothing owed to me, and to make it on the run, you gotta act as if you *ain't* on the run, 'cause the minute somebody get hip, it's a wrap, so take that for what its worth, homie...and by the way, happy birthday."

It was just yesterday that I walked out into the cold with a bag on my shoulder. Only this time the bag was filled with coke and 50,000 in cash! Damn! That nigga X been on the run for nineteen months. *Nineteen months*! Fuck what them niggaz is talking about, let me get nineteen months out this bitch and it's a fuckin' wrap!

While I waited for Victoria to get showered and changed, I looked around her apartment and saw pictures of her at her graduation, family pictures and pictures that I had sent to her while I was upstate, you know, the eight common jailhouse poses! I wondered what it would be like to live normally and come home to her every night. I liked the idea, but that wasn't an option right then because I had already renewed my contract with the game!

"Baby, are you hungry?" she asked as she came out with a thick white robe and had her head down as she was in the process of wrapping her hair in a white towel as most females do.

"Nah, I'm straight, but when you get a minute, I need to talk to you."

"Just give me a sec while I finish up in here," she hollered from her bedroom.

We sat on the couch and I told her with all sincerity, "You know I didn't want things to be this way. I wanted to be free, but not like this. I didn't want you to second guess the way I feel about you, but I want you to have a complete understanding of who I am. You following me?"

"Yeah, baby, I'm right here with you," she said.

I continued. "When I first met you, I thought that I could escape my reality and become a better man because of you and believe me, I have, but there are certain aspects of my life that as much as I try to shake them, I seem to easily fall victim to them, and no, I'm not talking about no other females."

She cut me off and said in a worried tone, "What's wrong, baby? Other than leaving that place, are you in trouble? Tell me so I can help."

I reached behind the couch and lifted the blue bag and decided that she should know. I emptied the contents of the bag onto the long oval shaped glass table in front of us and she grabbed onto my arm tighter than a woman would do on her date at a scary movie. She asked, "Baby, what did you do? What happened?"

I answered, "There ain't nothing to be worried about, and I didn't do anything that's gonna get me in trouble," I lied. "This was my life before I met you, before I went to prison and I guess in a way, you could say a few niggaz decided to pay homage and I got what was due to me, but you have absolutely nothing to worry about."

We were silent for a moment and she finally let go of my arm, reached over and touched the $50,000 and as she did, she asked, almost in a whisper, "Did you kill somebody?"

"Hell, no!" I replied. "This shit right there belongs to me and like I said, everything is everything, but this ain't the point of why I'm telling you and showing you this! You fell in love with me, *Anthony,* and I'm still *Anthony,* but what I need from you is to understand that this is a part of who I am and I love you enough to be honest with you about all of this. I love you enough to allow you to make the decision of whether or not you can deal with this. Do you love me enough, to love *all* of me?" I didn't know if I wanted the truth!

She went to the kitchen to get a light for the cigarette I held in my hand and when she returned, she lit my cigarette and walked around to the other side of the table. She picked up the blue bag and started to place all of the contents I poured onto the table back into the bag, looking at everything but me as she zipped the bag up.

I said, "Well? Don't I get an answer?"

What she did next blew my mind...she grabbed my hand and led me from the couch to the bedroom. She walked to the closet and put the blue bag in a space behind the wall and turned to me and said, "Anthony, I love you and the love I feel for you exceeds all logic and understanding because I came from a good family and went to college and I've never lived your type of lifestyle, that I *can't* understand completely, but baby, listen to me, that's the beauty and the power of what love really is! I'm on your team all the way and I ain't like none of these dizzy bitches out here. Sacrifice and support are second nature to me and baby, I appreciate your honesty, but if you let me, Daddy, I'll play my part to the fullest. I ain't going nowhere, not even when *you* choose to!"

I can't lie, I only thought that type of shit existed in movies and well-written books, but it was real and I had to close my eyes and reopen them to make sure! She was there and she was real! What does a man say after hearing something like that? How do you react to it? I definitely didn't know, so I pulled her into me and held her for what seemed like an eternity and said, "I love you, Ma...damn! I love you. And to think, I thought *I* had all the game," I said playfully as she slapped me in the arm.

Teasingly, she said, "Shut up, birthday boy...now open your present!"

I did exactly that as I pulled on the belt to her robe...and I spent my 24th birthday the only place I wanted to be and with the only person I wanted to be with! And to think, I didn't spend one dollar!

Chapter Four

T he first few months went by slowly because I had to get
back in tune with what was really going on in the world.
I never returned to the hotel, only once, the morning after
my birthday to get my things. I went against what I thought
to be my better judgement and moved in with Victoria for
two reasons. One, being that I felt safe with her and she
practically begged me and nobody knew about me and her,
not even the parole people!

Secondly, because I felt that regardless of how things
seemed to be going at first, that nigga J.O. wasn't who he
appeared to be and it's like the story goes with the old lady
and the snake. *The old lady saw a snake lying in the road dying
and out of loneliness, to benefit her needs, more so than the snake,
she took it home and nursed it back to good health. Every night
like clockwork for two months, she held the snake and petted it,
stroking it from front to back, and then one night she held the
snake and began to pet it as always and stroked it from back to
front and the snake turned around and bit her. As she was dying,
the said, "But why? I was your friend." The snake said, "Bitch,
you knew I was a snake when you brought me home!" She paid
with her life all because she rubbed the snake the wrong way!*

I knew this nigga was a snake and I refused to pay with my life *or* my freedom!

It took a week or two to get back in touch with the people I felt I needed to reach out to. Politics are a very important part of the *game*, and I was my very own campaign manager, and a good one at that.

I placed myself on a strict financial diet, telling myself that after struggling to make commissary upstate for so many years, and getting by, there wasn't any way in the world I couldn't stack my paper out here! I had that coke in the streets and ever since that day when I knocked on *opportunity's* door, I never once looked back. I had a few other *opportunities* and yeah, I took complete advantage of them, but after a while, it felt like a job and they seemed to get smaller and smaller financially, so I fell back because I was doing some eating to the point, that who knows, maybe one day a nigga might leave a halfway house and come knockin' on *my* door...besides, I was protected by V. No! Not Viper...*Victoria*. She hipped me to bank accounts and bonds and seven year investment mutual funds and all types of fly shit that I was ignorant to *once upon a time*.

My identification was solid in the system and everything thanks to an old friend of mines who was doing it up *real big* in Miami! Trini was a genius when it came to that type of thing amongst other things! Who knew that a nigga I met in prison, in the hole, would put me on with the best coke prices available. I didn't know how and I didn't care, but he came through!

I got a call the night before from Mei-Ling, X's financee'. We had been dealing with each other, me and X, for a minute on the coke tip and everything was going smoothly. Being on the run *together* as we always said, brought us a lot closer because X was a thoroughbred and he was always hungry *even* when he wasn't. He had been on the run for thirty-one months now. He just assumed they gave up looking, but he was always on point...unfortunately, according to Mei-Ling's phone call, he didn't have to run any more! He was found dead, inside of his Mercedes Benz yesterday morning with a hole in his hand and two in his neck and chest. She told me he was slumped over the steering wheel with his head on the horn, engine still running and his rims still spinning! They discovered a bag in the trunk of his car that contained one hundred, twenty-two thousand dollars in cash! A small contribution to the *Game Gods*.

I turned on the news...nothing...so I got dressed and went to the nearest gas station to get the paper. While I was there, I decided to get gas. A lady in a burgundy *S-Type* Jaguar was pulling out of the station smiling at me. I paid her no mind. Not that I wouldn't have liked to holla, but I had enough respect for Victoria to not play too close to home. Besides, there were more pressing matters on my mind! I walked out of the gas station after purchasing a paper and a bottle of coke and as I opened the door reading the paper, trying to locate the article that them muthafuckas at the newspaper company didn't find my man's death to be worthy of front page news, I bumped into some little ass nigga and kept it moving!

"A yo, my man, dig, where the fuck you going?" he said.

I was gonna keep it moving, but I had to see who the fuck would come out they face like that and as I did, a smile came to my face. "Oh, shit, it's a small muthafuckin' world and I don't know if it's built for two *big* niggaz! What's going on Big-Dee?"

Once he realized who I was, he said, "You nigga! Sometimes me! I see you doing big things," as he looked past me towards my means of transportation. A silver Lincoln Navigator with all the accessories to state my financial status amongst the ghetto-fabulous! One of the very few treats to myself.

I replied, "Man, this shit ain't about nothing. A nigga just trying to do a lil living while he still got the option to do it, you dig me?"

"That shit sounds good homie, and I might be working and playing that square role for these crackas, but I'm hip to what's going on around me, and nigga, you seem to be the talk of the town!"

"I ain't big on playing these streets too tough! I'm about to go get my mind right, but if you trying to ride, I'm definitely tryin' to get in your ear for a minute, so what's up?"

"Nah, I ain't busy with anything other than doing a whole lotta nothing, so let's ride nigga," he said as he entered the passenger side and we drove off.

I ain't really know where his head was at, so I took him to my young girl's spot, all the while giving him the impression that it's where I laid my head when I was in town.

When we arrived at Kia's house, she wasn't there as usual. I met La'Kia two months ago and decided she was worthy to keep on the side, 'cause for one, she was damn near next to gorgeous! And her head game was on 10,000! Besides the fact, I made my situation and status clear to her and I knew she was about money which was cool wit' me because it left out the demand for all the emotional aspects of a relationship. A little business mixed with pleasure, so to speak! Plus, I had a wifey!

I told Big-Dee that I came by the halfway joint a few times trying to reach him, but I wasn't comfortable being downtown. I told him that I talked to Evelyn a few times when I first bounced, but she was trying to get wifed by a nigga and I wasn't too much for it. That bitch was type dizzy!

"Yeah, I'm hip. That bitch switched her pitch up on me out of nowhere. They fired her stupid ass," he said.

"Word! What happened?" I asked.

"Man, the white boy that worked second shift came to work mad early one day, so he went to the third floor lobby and fell out before his shift started, and you know how the third floor lobby always be dead? Well, *Dizzy* and some new cat that just got there called themselves getting a lil *better acquainted*. Dig me, on the third floor and dude woke up and peeped game! The nigga, I think his name was TY, smashed out 'cause you know they was gon' lock 'em up and the broad got cut loose! I was loving that shit because the bitch got all funny style on me about letting my shorty through on the late night. Fuck dat' bitch!"

"A yo, you's a funny ass nigga!" I said. "So what you been doing out here as far as making it?" I liked this lil nigga and I wanted to feel him out a little.

"I was working at some nut ass factory but they was playing on the fact that they knew I needed them to *get by out here* type shit, so I bounced and I been working through this temp service on Lehigh, but they don't be half consistent as a nigga need 'em to be. That's where I just came from when I ran into you! Shit ain't easy at all out this bitch. One thing after the next, but yo, my shorty pregnant and a nigga been hustlin' a lil trees on the side, something small just to stay ahead a lil bit."

"Damn, nigga, you 'bout to have another seed?" I stated more than asked.

"Yeah, man, and my lil man about to be five already. I love my son yo, but honestly, I don't know if I'm built for two right now. Shit, I can barely do for one. You feel me?"

"Yeah, I feel you, homey!"

I changed the subject. "So, what you been hearing about the kid?" I was picking for info.

"I hear you doing big things, but I also hear you fuck wit' a nigga who ain't really riding wit' you and from what I hear, that nigga supposed to be..." he stopped mid-sentence and said, "yo, I ain't the type of nigga to knock nobody hustle, you feel me, but I fucks wit' you and I couldn't really acknowledge you as my man if I ain't give you what's good, so I'ma be straight up wit' you. I ain't ever met the kid, J.O., but word is, that niggaz hotter than fish grease and I'm talking 'bout *dealing wit' them boys*, and a few niggaz is up north about that cat! I don't know how true it is, but that's the word, my nigga, and truthfully, some of these niggaz out here feel that's why you and that nigga eating like that."

He looked away from me awaiting my response. I had heard lil rumors, but I know this nigga! He had snake in 'em no doubt, but playing police, nah! I knew this nigga since we was kids, so I said, "Yo, muthafuckas is bitches and you know a bitch always need something to rap about! Dog, not that I feel the need to justify myself, but me, I ain't ever and I mean *EVER* play the other side of the fence. And..."

He cut me off noticing the seriousness in my tone and said, "Ant, I know better, homey, and that's why I'm telling you and not running around feeding into that shit behind ya back. I been trying to get up wit' you for a minute too, but we always missing each other, but niggaz ain't saying you on it like that. They say ya man type funny and his status keeps you safe and protected. Niggaz even said that ya man ain't really feeling you like that, but you came home and knew how to do what he and a lot of muthafuckas couldn't do for years in a matter of months and the only reason he ain't crossed you up is 'cause he feel obligated about how you held him down for the eight years you put in for 'em!" He looked directly at me awaiting a response.

"So you telling me that the nigga a "Hot Boy," and he feel obligated to me! Ain't no such thing as a halfway snake. Grimy is through and through and I'm hip to the fact that the nigga ain't feeling me, but it's important for a nigga to keep his enemies closer than his friends and I ain't gonna sign no check and say the nigga *ain't* hot, but at the same time, I can't go by some rap, and condemn 'em either! I appreciate you putting me on for real, Dee, and the only thing I can really do is play the nigga close again and do what's best for me! As soon as I figure that shit out, whatever the choice is, it gotta be mines! You feel me?"

He shook his head and said, "I ain't saying nothing as far as what the nigga is and what he ain't 'cause like I said, I don't know him, but I know you and you one of the very few niggaz who did what you said you was gonna do, and truth be told, nigga, you a dying breed. Do what you gotta do, playa, just stay on point!" He fell into a deep thought for a minute and said, "Yo, as a matter of fact, I think I seen that kid before. Do he drive a black on black ES?"

I replied, "Yeah."

He continued. "I don't know if it was the kid J.O. or not, but I saw this nigga down on Second the night before last getting fucked around by some light skinned cat! I was fucking wit' this shorty down there and she knew the nigga with the ES and was saying, *That's good for that nigga*, but she said his name was..."

I cut him off and ended the sentence, "Cypher." "Yeah, yeah, that's the name right there. That's the same nigga?"

"Yeah, that's him! You say he got fucked around? What happened?" I asked.

"I don't really know, but it was mad late and by the time we got to the window, ya man was falling up the steps of the spot across the street trying to get away from the nigga. Yo, kid gripped 'em up and hit 'em wit a joint and everything and put that shit right in his mouth and said something, and next thing I knew, while he was pointing the joint at ya man, he jumped up and got in the ES and smashed out!"

"So that's why I ain't seen this nigga in a few days! Damn! Who was the nigga that fucked him around like that?" I asked.

"Some light skinned nigga! I don't be knowing these cats like that on no personal level, but I seen the kid a few times. I ain't know he was getting it like that though," he said.

"What you mean 'getting' it?'" I asked.

"Yo, once ya man left, the light skinned kid hopped in a white big body Benz and was out."

I lost focus for a minute! I didn't wanna believe what I was hearing! It had to be another nigga with the white Benz down on Second! I glanced over at the paper sitting on the table and immediately knew that I was trying to deny the fact, that X was the light skinned cat in the Benz! I told myself *regardless of what happened down on the block, these niggaz knew each other longer than I knew either of them. Whatever beef they had, I know it ain't come down to this! What could they have been beefing over! Damn!*

"A yo, Ant, somebody at the door, fam."

My train of thought was broken as Dee looked toward the door.

"Breath easy," I said. "That's just my shorty!"

La'Kia walked in the house with a curious look on her face and I understood, because I never brought anybody over there other than members of my immediate team, so to set her mind at ease, I said, "Kia, this my man *Komplete*.

Big-Dee looked at me and was right on point, as he said, "How you doing, uh...?"

Trying to think if he had caught her name right, or at least that's what I thought, so I said, "Kia."

"Yeah, Kia, how you doing?" he said.

She came right in and sat down next to me and started to get into a conversation about a whole bunch of nothing.

I turned towards her and gave her a look that basically told her without saying that she was out of place, even in her home and should know *her* role! She got hip real quick and excused herself.

"You gon' have to excuse shorty, she type *jo-jo* familiar," I said. "You know how that goes, especially wit' females."

My mind was racing and I knew everything he had told me and the situation with X had to be addressed, but to sit and debate with him about *what's what* and *who's who* within my team would be fruitless right then. It was *my* problem, because it was *my* team.

"C.F.I.," yeah, that was my thing! Me, X, J.O., Ani-Dog, Double-M, a.k.a. Murdah Mo, Kwon, Ant-Live, Y.T., a.k.a. Yung Thug! We all came up together down on Second Street, the livest block in the city! The block represented so many things, and taught a nigga the meaning of *Survival of the Fittest*. The grimy atmosphere created and groomed some of the best that ever done it and at the same time, it consumed a lot of good niggas, either by death or worse, the system! I hustled back then for the sake of gettin' by and learned so many things down there about life, about this game, and I fell in love, literally, with the *Game*. That block was my home, it was my special place in this big world! I made a name for myself real quick, and fast, trying to have my hand in any and every thing, and more so, by being the go-to. That was the person you could go to if you saw a way to come up, and I would figure out and find a way to make it happen, and more importantly, I was more than willing to be on the front line!

On the block, there were a lot of different squads that even though they held it down for *Second*, they represented each other on a more extreme level and we decided that our title had to represent *us*, so we came up with "C.F.I.," which stood for "Crime Family Incorporated." We were most definitely about that crime, and we were family without all the titles, cousins, brothers, etc., and the "Incorporated" part at that time sounded major, real important and we all planned to be exactly that! *C.F.I. till we die*. It's a shame, but for some of us, that's what it actually came down to, some sooner than later, but this, the most promised part of living was...dying!

Sometimes, when I think of my homies that ain't make it and gave their lives to this shit, I feel guilty! Maybe if I wasn't in prison all them years, I might have been able to change something! Who knows? Then I think I let prison save me from what *might have, could have*, and sometimes, I feel *should have* been my fate!

I can remember a time when hustling and everything that came with it was fun! It's almost as if...*just like that*...in a blink of an eye, the whole game changed. Like everybody traded in the smiling faces, and when things got a lil outta hand, they traded in a fair one, for, ice grills and burners! DAMN! House parties! Roller rinks! When the fuck did that shit become lame? Girls became bitches! Too much money, made a *once upon a time friendship* funny! Shit. When was the last time I saw a muthafucka smoke a joint? I don't even smoke no more for the same reasons I once did. I smoke to try and escape *now*!

I ain't really in no position to be complaining though 'cause I could have made my mind up to walk away from this shit just as easily as I chose to walk away from that fucking halfway house, and at least made an attempt to square-up, but I guess that I'm afraid of what I don't know and I damn sure don't know the square life! It can't really be that I'm afraid to fail, because I was born into this life. I didn't choose it, this game chose me and I've been trying all my life to win, but I ain't been doing nothing but losing...friends *and* time! I made my mind up though, that it's time to really apply myself and win for a change! Right now, I just gotta take my time and figure out how to go about doing that!

Too much was happening too fast! *Why the fuck X gotta be dead? This wasn't part of my plans at all. Shit!* What was it that nigga used to always say?...Oh, yeah! He used to say, *"Nigga, I do me 'cause truthfully, I ain't afraid to die! This shit gets harder every fuckin' day and it's living too long that I fear!"*...Up until now. I could never bring myself to even completely understand the logic behind that. I can't say that I agree, but I do understand where he was coming from! *Why now though?* We were *finally* doing some eating for real! We were in the process of making our dreams a fuckin' reality!

Please don't let there be any truth to the shit Big-Dee told me earlier!...That's all I could think about as I drove home, to Victoria. I had a lot on my mind and I really needed to be comforted and consoled! I needed to be with the one person I felt I could trust. I needed to cry! Something I hadn't done in years! I needed to cry, not so much for my friend X, alone, but for all of my homies! For Ani-Dog, serving fifteen to thirty upstate. For Ant-Live and Y.T., both serving twenty to forty years, and for Double-M for living up to his name, serving two consecutive life sentences...life...for all of the things we missed out on and would never have the opportunity to experience. Even for Kwon, who was smart enough to walk away from all this shit and go hard on the legal side of things! Mostly for J.O. for being grimy and going against the grain and for what I would eventually have to do, to right all of his wrongs, if what I've been told to be the truth comes to manifest itself...*Please! Don't let there be any truth to the shit Big-Dee told me today.*

As I stood in the doorway with that distant look in my eye, Victoria came to the door and said, "Baby, what's wrong?"

As I stood there in a daze, at war with my thoughts, trying to fight what I knew was reality, I couldn't find the words so I responded, "What's right?"

Chapter Five

"**B**aby, you know you really don't have to go if you ain't feeling up to it! You did more than your share and if the police are gonna be there, like you said, why you gonna take that risk?"

"Yeah, I'm hip, but I gotta pay my respects! I *need* to be there! I don't wanna see my nigga like that, but if it was me, I know he would've been there." I told Victoria, as I continued to dress, I knew the police were gonna be there, but it really didn't make a difference. I personally felt that that was gonna be a violation of my man X's funeral, but police always gotta be police and as many times as I've been stopped already by them crackas, they weren't worrying about me. They were looking for suspects and I wasn't him! I wasn't the fucking police, but I was doing the exact thing...*looking for reactions and suspects*! Only, they wouldn't be held accountable in no fuck ass court of law!

As we entered the church down on Front Street, which I chose because it was the closest to home, our home, Second Street, I thought it would be appropriate, I noticed people that I hadn't seen in years. People who I didn't even think would care, but they were there to pay their respects. I smiled on the inside from the thought of it!

X's family was non-existent other than his son, Tariq, and Mei-Ling. I wondered if these same people would attend my funeral or if anybody would...I guess, only time would tell. I saw J.O. talking to Kwon and everything just seemed real normal. Our conversation from the day after X got killed played in my mind, again, like it's been doing for the past few days. Something told me I had to call the nigga J.O. and I'm glad that I did, but then again, I'm not! Truth hurts!

"Hello," J.O. answered.

"A yo, what's good, homie?" I said as calm and peaceful as I could.

"Man, I can't call it. What's good wit' you?"

"I'm about to get touched wit' that Miami Heat! I'm trying to see where we at, so try and get wit' me before tonight, aiight?"

"Yeah, most definitely! I been waiting on you," he said.

"Dig right, I don't know about the nigga X," I said in search of some type of funny reaction. I wanted the nigga to think I wasn't hip to what happened yet. "He was supposed to get up wit' me yesterday and I ain't heard from or seen that nigga in like three days now! Yo, you think them people bagged the nigga on that nut ass escape shit?"

"Yo, no bullshit! I was thinking the same muthafuckin' thing yesterday!" he said.

"Why you say that?"

"'Cause, I ain't seen or heard from the nigga myself in..." he paused to give the impression of deep thought before he continued..."shit, it's been about a week now and that ain't like him to stay away from family! Dig me?"

Family, huh? I couldn't believe the nigga said that shit! I checked up on the situation that Dee told me about! He even brought shorty over that he was with and she gave me everything! Bitches talk, but shorty took it to a whole nother level. She knew me, but unfortunately, there weren't too many who didn't. She wasn't hip to why she was there because I ain't want it to seem like I was snooping around, but I knew that a couple shots of this and that, and some good green would open up the gossip highway and everybody knew that me, X and J.O. were peoples. It didn't take long at all!

She said, "Ant, I'm sorry 'bout what happened wit' ya man! It's a shame, but I knew it was gonna happen. My girl, Deana, told me that Cypher and X were going through it for a while now over some work the nigga passed off to X that was some bullshit."

"She told you what?" I said, well, asked, in a more curious tone than a surprised one.

"Yeah, she said X came to her spot last Tuesday and he was in his feelings talkin' 'bout how J.O. tried to get over on him asking him to do him a favor and move the shit for him, but it was no good and X ain't wanna put his name on the shit, because it was too much money to be lost."

"So what happened with that shit?" I asked.

"Ant, why you playing? You the fuckin' man out here, and them your boyz, so what you think happened wit' it? Didn't you come up short this week?"

I did, but it wasn't none of her fucking business and I was gonna tell her so, but the broad was offering too much intel for next to nothing. So I dummied up on her and said, "Short? Ma', you got me fucked up! I don't get down no more. Them days is over. I just fuck wit' niggaz wit' a popular rep."

She rolled her eyes and said, "Anyway, what happened to that shit don't even matter. Besides, it would only be relevant to a boss." She said that shit sarcastically, but I wasn't even gonna jump out there, so she went on. "I don't know what happened in detail, but a few nights ago, they was trying to go on each other in the club and I'm assuming it was about that money and Cypher said the next time they crossed paths, anything goes, and then late that night, we saw X giving the nigga the blues and, well you know..."

Yeah, I definitely knew! I just didn't know why I wasn't on point wit' all that shit!

I had every intent on giving the nigga the blues myself, but now wasn't the time! He walked around the church and spoke to everybody and if I ain't know any better, I would have thought he really *did* care, 'cause his acting was on *one thousand*! I was about to go over to him, and just before I was in motion, Kwon grabbed my arm and when I looked at him, all I saw was pain in his eyes! It's almost as if he was trying to tell me so with his eyes, but how could *he* know?

He said, "We speeding homie! We all gon' get there! Why we gotta rush?"

I knew what he was saying, but I couldn't even respond. Kwon was like my big brother and I always listened when he had something to say. When Ant-Live and Y.T. got bagged, it took a lot from him and he decided that this shit just wasn't for him anymore. *"Too much gun play and drama,"* is what he said. I wasn't feeling that shit at all, not so much that he meant what he said, because I knew he planned to do it, but because I wished I had the heart to walk away and listen to him this time, like all the times before, but I was too lost in my ways to do it. I was *grown folks*! I even tried to clown the nigga on some square shit, but it was my envy that spoke for me and he told me, he knew it! I introduced him to Victoria and after we spoke for a while, we promised to get up with each other real soon and more frequently! I would've liked it, but I doubted it!

The service was more than I expected! I saw my homie X for the last time and told him that I'd miss him! That I missed him already! To stay a soldier and don't do no compromising! It's too late for that! I told him that I would look out for Tariq and the way it seemed, I'd see him again soon, but I promised on everything that I loved that I'd be sending some company his way sometime in the near future...and before I walked away, I put a picture I had of him and me from when we were eleven years old out front of his grand-mom's house trying to stunt, into his hand and said, "C.F.I. til' we die. Rest in peace, homie, 'cause there's no peace in war." In life we were at war.

I left after that and took Victoria home. We rode in complete silence the whole way, and when we pulled up into the driveway, she saw that I had no intention of getting out of the car, so she broke the ice and said, "Anthony, why don't you come and lay down, relax your mind a lil bit? Them streets ain't going nowhere."

When I declined and told her I had to see a few people, she broke on me! As she spoke, she started to cry and I knew it was to come. I just wished that it didn't have to be on *that* day, at *that* moment especially! She said, "Until today, I've never in my life been to a funeral! I went because I wanted to support you and a part of me wanted to see that other part of your life up close and personal. I love you, and truthfully, that's really an understatement, and I mean that. Anthony, I don't wanna ever have to attend another funeral! Ever! You came out here and accomplished so much in such a little amount of time, but baby, I don't understand exactly what it is you feel you need to prove. I don't know who you feel you need to prove it to! We can leave here! Anywhere you wanna go! Please, Anthony, look at me...don't make me attend another funeral!"

"Listen to me," I said, as I turned off the engine. "In a perfect world, I could promise you that you won't ever have to attend a funeral! All I can say is, in a minute, things are gonna change, either for the better or the worse, and they're definitely gonna change! I don't ever want you to feel that I'm forcing your hand. You don't have to feel obligated about anything! Everything I've done for you, and everything I do for you is out of love. You never have to question that! Now, if you feel that you can't deal with this shit anymore, you tell me where you tryin' to go and I'll put you there, just say the word, but don't sit there and expect me to switch my pitch up this late in the game 'cause this shit's getting too explicit for your eyes."

I reached for her hands and she pulled away. Before she could even attempt to respond I said, "That shit right there ain't gonna get us nowhere! I'm trying to give you what nobody gave me and that's a chance to not have to attend funerals, a chance to walk away with some stability! Tori, this shit ain't for you! It ain't even for me, but it's all that I know! For the past few months, I've been seeing the changes in you and I don't wanna hurt you anymore. Baby, I'd rather be blind than to continue to see you in pain! Walk away from me while you can and when I do figure all this shit out, there's nothing, and I mean nothing, that will keep me from you!"

She allowed me to grab her hands this time and she asked, "Why do I have this feeling telling me this is something you've been thinking about? I don't want you to make any noble gestures at my expense! How the hell am I supposed to just up and leave you? It's not that easy! Baby, I'm not going anywhere, and I don't want you to go anywhere! At least not tonight, just stay with me!" As she eased the keys out of the ignition and began to get out of the car, I couldn't argue with her, so I followed suit...*tomorrow always promised to be another day!*

A few weeks had passed and with X no longer here, I found myself in the company of Big-Dee a lot more often. He helped me tie up a few loose ends and proved himself to be worthy, so in turn, I handed him the reins to what was once X's share and responsibility. X had dealt with a team of grimy niggaz, but they manifested loyalty and knew that alone, they would be *in the way* more than *on* the way! Everybody couldn't be a boss, and they understood that and for the time being, were content with their status.

For political and business purposes, I continued to deal with J.O. and it wasn't easy to refrain from emptying a clip into his face each and every time I saw him, but it was necessary to play my part because I was in the process of building an empire on the foundation of what I believed in, and I was determined to make it happen and as much as I despised the nigga, he played a vital role in this shit, but his time was coming, and I was the only one who knew it! With that, I was one step ahead!

Over the course of the next three months, I decided that it was time to really start treating myself, because life was too short to be cheating myself! I brought two new houses and allowed Victoria and Kia to decorate each to their liking and they both did exactly that. It kept them busy and I felt bad about allowing Kia access to all of that, but as much as my heart belonged to Victoria, by that time I was caught up and Kia was five-and-a-half months pregnant and home was where I laid my head, and I always wanted to be comfortable!

For Victoria's birthday I bought her a brand new purple CLK 430 Benz with our names engraved in the dash and stitched into the headrest and I purchased a few vehicles of my choice, a Range Rover and a BMW 745i, burgundy. I didn't put a whole lot of work into them because at that time, just having them seemed to be enough!

Yeah, everything seemed to be going my way, and other than a little drama here and there, business was beautiful! For the first time in a long time, I got that reassuring feeling that this shit was worth it!

When I answered my phone, I was definitely pleased to hear the voice on the other line..."Trini-Mon, what's good?" I said with enthusiasm because I knew that a call from him, instead of to him, was always good, especially for business!

He said, "You! Sometimes me! But mostly you! How's everything going, my friend?"

"Honestly, everything is good and I mean everything! As we speak, I'm sitting here getting a manicure by the prettiest gift God gave to man and she's blessing me with the best manicure I've ever had." I winked at shorty and on cue, she smiled and blushed. I wasn't really lying, she was giving me a good manicure! The rest was good for public relations! She was public and in the words of Bill Clinton, *"I did plan to have relations with her."*

"So what's on your mind?" I asked.

"It's a strange story! Last night I had a dream I was on a plane. Today, I ended up here! I figure everything happens for a reason and I couldn't think of a better reason to be on a plane than to be in the presence and company of a very good friend, so what's on the agenda, my friend?"

"I know that's right," I said. "As far as the agenda, I'm on my way to see a good friend too."

He understood that I was on my way to see him A.S.A.P. at the usual spot. I hated the drive, but it was always worth it! Trini had gotten hooked on some young girl I introduced him to a while back. So much so that he put her in a brand new house, everything paid for and called it *home away from home*. I called it *whipped*, but who was I to complain...*The closest get the mostest.*

I called J.O. and Big-Dee and informed them that I would be inactive for a few hours and that I needed them to make rounds and make sure everything was good!

As I arrived at Trini's *home away from home*, shorty greeted me at the door and asked me to wait in the back by the pool. She offered me a drink and I declined. I didn't like this part of my visits here because Trini always liked to be dramatic and enter the stage on *his* time!

But fuck it, he earned that right!

About ten minutes had passed, and I was beginning to get irritated, when Trini decided to finally grace me with his presence.

"My friend, it's been some time," he stated.

"Most definitely! Too long to be exact! So, to what exactly do I owe this honor?"

"In due time...have a drink with me and let's discuss a few things before we rush into business! We are friends, are we not?" He nodded with a drink in his hand.

"Without question! What's on your mind?" I asked.

"I like to keep my eyes and ears open," he began, "and because I am not able to be, unfortunately, everywhere at once, I have people who are paid very well to do so for me! My eyes and ears have informed me of your most recent mishap and the loss of a friend can never be healthy for business, although you've proven otherwise financially. A fool reacts off of emotions and that, my friend, could be very bad for business! I am aware of the fact that *Jermaine Owens* or *J.O.* as you would refer to him, is responsible for your recent loss and I'm also aware of the fact that you already knew this. As your friend and business associate, I would like to offer you two things! First and foremost, I would like to offer you the services of another good friend of mines who is..." he stopped as though he were in deep thought..."how can I say," he continued..."in a position to make your problem go away, so to speak. Secondly, I would like to offer you some advice, because I know you well, and I know that my first offer will never be accepted by you."

He stood and watched me, searching for my reaction

and he definitely knew me. I made a promise to a *friend* that I was truly a man of my word! So I said, "I hear you," and he continued.

"My advice to you is to continue to be patient and always allow opportunity to present itself to you. When you choose to do what's best for you, *trust no one* and the best witness is a dead witness!"

"Trini, I appreciate your advice and believe me, I am taking it for what it's worth. I've always valued your opinion so it's worth a lot! Know this here, I'm gonna allow nothing to come between what it is we're doing, so you can rest assured that this paper is top priority! You feel me?"

"That's exactly what I wanted to hear. With that said and done, let me explain my reason for coming so unexpectedly and in person."

I knew it was what he wanted to hear and I meant every word of it! He knew it too! He said, "You have proven to be worthy of your request of fifty kilos a month. Your ticket is 9.5, and I hope that we can continue to do good business for a long time! Oh, yeah, one more thing, my eyes and ears also tell me that the Iranians have attempted to begin talks with you..."

Damn! This muthafucka was like *Screwface...everywhere.* He saw the surprise in my eyes and went on.

"In this business, it is good to have friends, but worse to have true enemies! They are no good for business! Leave them alone!" he said more as a demand than anything and I wasn't slow, I caught the threat even though he said all of the above in a humble tone with a smile!

"I got you, Trini...I definitely got you on that!" I said as I raised my glass to his and said, "To business," to which he said, "To friendship!"

I drove home and gave some good thought to our conversation and I knew that as much as one man can and will acknowledge another as a *friend*, money can and will come between that. X was proof of that!

Chapter Six

It's said that *the only thing that comes to those who sleep...are dreams!* I only wish I could be so fortunate!

All the excitement of the day's events with Trini took its toll on me and I found myself resting my eyes and before I knew it, sound asleep!

I opened my eyes and immediately closed them, almost afraid to open them because I couldn't believe what I was seeing!

"Wake up, nigga!" I heard a voice say. "Come on, man, get your ass up!"

I knew the voice all too well, but I knew it had to be a dream. As I opened my eyes, X was standing over top of me smiling as he said, "Welcome home, nigga, I see its gonna take some time for you to get used to that dro', come on man, you sleeping through your own party!"

I couldn't believe it, but it was happening. Everybody was there! Y.T., Ani-Dog, J.O., Double-M, Kwon, Ant-Live, even Big-Dee and Victoria! Everybody was all smiles.

I got my head right and I looked at my homie and said, "A party? Why you're throwing me a party? Yo, X, what's going on?"...I reached out to grab his arm. *Was it real?*

He just laughed and said, "A yo, Tori, you better come get ya man, he all delusional and shit! Here, nigga, drink this." He handed me a Corona and I drank it immediately!

Victoria came over to me, looking at me through eyes that I hadn't seen in a long time. There was no pain! "Hey, baby! Don't worry, you didn't sleep through much, so you didn't miss anything." She sat on the armrest and kissed me on my forehead.

"Baby, this shit seems too real! What are they doing here? I mean, how?" I asked.

"They're your boys. They wanted to throw you a party for your birthday and to welcome you home and I was invited, eventually! What's wrong?"

I know I was trippin' but for the time being, everything seemed worth it. J.O. and Y.T. were over by the door talking with Big-Dee and Ani-Dog, and they were laughing and carrying on like old times, except for the fact that I never knew Big-Dee to know Ani-Dog. But everything seemed so real and I didn't want it to end, so I replied, "Nothing, baby, everything is right! Everything's alright! Let me go holla at these niggaz before they get the impression that your man can't hang."

I smiled and walked over to the door slowly, hoping that it was real and that I wouldn't blink and it would be all over. As I approached them, I said, "What's good fellas?" Nobody responded so I figured with the music being so loud, they just ain't hear me, so I repeated myself. "Damn! You niggaz deaf? I said what's good fellas?" They just continued talking as if I wasn't even there!

I felt a hand on my shoulder and I looked back and X was standing there. "They can't hear you, homie."

"Fuck you mean, they can't hear me? Yo, go ahead with the jokes niggaz, what's good?" I yelled at the top of my lungs! Still no response!

"Dig yourself! They can't speak to the dead, my nigga."

"Yo, X, what the fuck is going on?"

"You ain't handle ya business, dog, so I handled you."

"What you trying to say, I'm dead or something?"

He looked at me and I knew the answer. I continued to ask questions. "So how come you can hear me, and what about Victoria, how come she can see and hear me?"

"Come on, nigga, you ain't forget that fast did you? You know my situation, but as far as Tori, I hate to be the bearer of bad news," he drifted off for a second and then said, "she's a casualty of war, my nigga!"

I searched the room for her, but she wasn't there. "We made it," he said, "we made it, Ant."

"We made it where?"

"To hell, dog! Welcome home!"

I closed my eyes hoping to wake up, but it was just too fuckin' real, and when I opened them, I saw X standing there shaking his head staring at me through disappointed eyes.

"X, why is Victoria here? Yo, she ain't ever done nothing! Shit don't make no sense."

"She's just in limbo, dog! She's chasing you, and she don't even know it herself yet."

I ran through the house, searching for Victoria, yelling her name, but there was no response, so I ran out the door. I saw her! I ran down the street chasing her and when I turned into the small side street, there she was, sitting on a curb with her head in her lap. As I approached her, I said, "Baby, don't run from me. I didn't know! I really didn't know."

She lifted her head and just that quickly it wasn't her anymore. It was Tariq, X's son, sitting there with tears in his eyes, and to my surprise, a .45 in his hands. He looked up at me as he pointed the gun in my direction and said, "You promised my daddy, you promised him."

I took a step towards him and an explosion stopped me

in my tracks...I looked down and my hands were gripping my stomach and as the blood began to ease through my fingers, I felt the warmth and the heat. I looked up from my hands and everybody was there, shaking their head in disappointment. I didn't understand! I asked, "Why?"

"Boy, what's wrong with you? Wake up!...Ant, wake up!"

I was never more happy to see La'Kia in all the time that I knew her. I threw the covers off of me and reached down for my stomach. Relieved, I smiled at her and said, "Come over here and let me kiss my baby," reaching out for her stomach.

She stood there and said, "Only if you promise to kiss me too."

Even as she stood there at the edge of the bed five-and-a-half months into her pregnancy, she was still intoxicating and so, so sexy! As I kissed her stomach, she held my head and my mind wandered back to my dream, or my nightmare, and I didn't wanna think about it anymore and I was afraid to close my eyes, fearing the possibility of another! I know there's a reason for everything and I knew I would have to answer to my subconscious, and I promised I would, but not right then. Not at that moment...in due time...

* * * * * * * *

"Your business *is* my business. What's good?"

"That's a hell of a way to answer your phone, nigga. That flamboyant shit ain't what's up!" I said in response to J.O. answering his phone.

"We too deep now to be on some ol' paranoid shit. What's the deal?" he asked.

"True! But niggaz ain't got to be slopping wit' this shit either! Anyway, I need to get in your head for a minute sometime before the day is through."

"What's on your mind, dog?" he asked in a more serious tone.

"You know I ain't real loose wit' the phone thing and everything ain't for everybody, so when you finish handling your B.I., meet me at the spot downtown. Hit me when you on your way."

"Yo, everything alright?" he asked more curious than concerned.

"Everything's everything," I commented.

"Alright...one!" he said.

"One."

I had read somewhere once to *keep your friends close and your enemies closer*. As of recently, I hadn't been taking heed to it and one thing about this nigga J.O. was he ain't ever been accused of being a dumb nigga! Everything he did was with reason and purpose and the other day he introduced me to some nigga out of his squad and that was never supposed to happen. I wanted to know why it did.

Maybe he was right. Maybe I was paranoid because over the course of the last two months, I ain't even feel comfortable meeting this nigga unless it was in a public place. Maybe I was paranoid about what he might try to do to me or maybe I was afraid of what I might want to do to him! Either way, its better to be safe than sorry! My dream was weighing heavy on my mind and I wasn't no damn interpreter or anything like that, but I knew what X meant when he said, *my business took care of me*. Keep my enemies close!

Sometimes I wondered what this shit was all about. Life wasn't supposed to be this way at all! Complicated was one word to describe it. I can still close my eyes sometimes and smell the inside of the Boys Club. I could remember how we were always getting into something and back then we had no worries for real. Death and prison weren't even a part of our vocabulary. We borrowed each other's clothes and never thought twice about it. I could just imagine me borrowing an outfit from a nigga now! Wouldn't that be something? I couldn't wait to get older and I really didn't know why, but it just seemed like the thing to be and if I only knew then, damn! There's no getting those times back and as insignificant as they may seem, life was never better! Never! I'd give it all up in a minute to be able to think and feel like I did then. Carefree is a good word to describe it! Right now, I feel like I'm all alone in that Boys Club swimming pool, right in the middle with water barely above my chin and I'm on my toes, jumping up and down to keep from going under and no one's there. I'm trying to reach the edge, in any direction, to get out, but I'm stuck. I'm yelling for help, but nobody's there to hear me. It's 3 a.m. and I'm not supposed to be in there, but I had to be different. I'm drowning and nobody is watching or maybe they just can't see me. Maybe I'm insignificant!

"Peace! What's good?" I said, as I answered my phone.

"I'm on my way...fifteen minutes, alright?"

"Peace!"

The Art Gallery was my spot downtown. Peaceful, quiet and interesting! I looked at the paintings and attempted to decipher what the artists were thinking of. The paintings were ugly as hell, but beautiful and captivating at the same time. Not so much the paintings themselves, but what they represented in my eyes...*Power!* People I knew didn't buy art and they damn sure didn't frequent any art galleries. No, the people who did, the people who were in a position to pay these astronomical figures did so, not because they were beautiful, but to own them gave each individual a sense of social status higher than the next. I mean, what's pretty about the *Mona Lisa*? What's beautiful about abstract art? The beauty is being in a position to purchase those sorts of things and not think twice about it. Money represented power to the fullest!

"Man, you and these damn pictures! Let me find out

this paper going to your head and you trying to get all ritzy and shit." J.O. said as he appeared on the pillar.

"Nah, I ain't on it like that! If it ain't afrocentric and almost cheap, it ain't for me! I only contribute to causes worthy of being contributed to!"

"So what's popping, my nigga? What's on your mind?"

I hesitated before I began, and finally I said, "You remember when we were kids? When we used to always rap about this type of shit, having all the money, clothes, cars and bitches?"

He laughed a little and said, "Do I ever."

"Did you think it would be like this?" I asked wondering myself.

"Be like what?" I seemed to have his full attention at this point.

"I mean, we on our way, there's no doubt about that, but look what we left behind. This thing is real serious and it's not even about survival anymore. Shit, it never was, but it damn sure ain't what it was supposed to be! Don't get me wrong, I ain't complaining 'cause I know it could be worse, but look at us, we all we got left and we have to set up meetings and shit just to rap," I confessed.

"Yeah! I'm hip! But you know if the shit was like we wanted it to be, it would be too much like right and you know how that go. Time nigga! Time changes things and things change with time. It's inevitable! I feel what you trying to say, but man, it's a cold world and a nigga gotta bundle up the best way he know how 'cause only the strong survive and this right here," he said as he patted his waistline, indicating that he had his burner on him, "this right here is all the heat I need 'cause me, I ain't got nothing else and I plan to survive, my nigga!"

"I miss them, yo," I expressed.

"You miss who?"

"Everybody! X, Y.T., Ani-Dog, Live, Mo, everybody! I be feeling guilty sometimes 'cause all this was for them too. You feel me?"

"You know I ain't big on these type of conversations, but for what it's worth, yeah, I feel you, but everybody made choices, everybody took chances, fate is fate and we here, so we gotta do what we can to keep ours from being so harsh, you feel me?"

"Besides all that, what's on your mind?" He sounded impatient and irritated.

I wasn't feeling anything the nigga said! I was trying to give him a chance to say something! Anything that would cause me to feel that he wasn't the business that *needed to be handled*, but optimism wasn't ever one of my strong points, but I was trying! Believe me, I was trying. "We doing big things, but we about to step this shit up another notch or two and I need you to know where my head is at. It's one thing to have it, like the havers have it, but it's another to keep it like the keepers keep it! We got a whole lot done in next to no time, but you know as well as I do that tomorrow ain't promised and when I get what it is I need to get, I'm falling back, way back!"

"What you mean...falling back?" he asked, almost shocked.

"Niggas ain't living right! I put plenty work in and it's always business. I'm trying to do what's best for me and enjoy the fruits of this labor! Like you said, 'everybody took their chances,' and I'm taking mines before I ain't got one to take. I ain't saying this is it 'cause I ain't ready for all that, but I'm just putting you on point," I said.

"So you just gonna up and leave all this shit like it ain't nothing? Yo, you a grown man and if that's how you feel, cool! But what about right now? It's a lot of muthafuckas depending on you to play your part, so how you think that shit's gonna sit with them?" He tried to put all the weight of the world on my shoulders, but mentally, I was as strong as an ox.

"Like I said, it ain't over yet! I'm just letting you know because *we* made this what it is, and knowing what I told you places you a few steps ahead of the rest."

"Alright, now what?"

"Now we get rich, my nigga! What I'm telling you is for you. We gotta put our heads together and know that shit is changing. Thus far, we've been blessed. There's no room for mistakes. I wanna ease my way to the back in about six months so I don't wanna meet anybody else!" I informed. "Yo, the other day you introduced me to your mans and we already spoke about that shit."

"Who, Deals and Danger? They good people," J.O. tried to convince me.

"Dig right, I ain't disputing whether they're *good peoples* or not. That ain't the point. The point is that they're *your* people, not mines and I don't trust nobody that ain't family. You feel me? 'Cause it only takes one bad muthafucka to bring down a whole lot of good ones and I can't afford it."

"That was my bad! It didn't seem like no big thing at the time, but yo, I would never put you on nobody that was sheisty. You feel me?" J.O. said trying to make things right.

"Yeah, I feel you." I didn't, but I agreed anyway.

"Good."

We walked towards the entrance preparing to go our separate ways and as he walked toward his car, he looked back and said, "Yo, Ant."

"What up?" I responded.

"You my nigga?" he asked in a question form.

"Nah! I'm your brother! Remember that!" I winked at him and kept it moving.

I drove around for a while thinking about the conversation he and I just had. I knew he wasn't hearing me, but I was trying to feel him out. His eyes and actions said ten times more than his words, and I didn't like any of it!

Three hours of driving and thinking! Thinking and driving! I'd been stalling for too long now. It wasn't the easiest thing in the world to deal with. *How do you build up the courage to kill your brother?* I guess I should have asked him that! I pulled up to my driveway and sat there for a minute. I closed my eyes and said out loud, "Damn X, I don't know what to do, homie. Help me, I know you hear me." As I got out of the car and headed towards the door, my phone went off. It was J.O. telling me how he meant to holla earlier but the conversation we had was unexpected and it slipped his mind. He wanted me to do him a favor!

"What type of favor?" I asked him.

"I'm on the highway right now, headed to the city to handle some things. My youngbuck, you know the nigga *Na'feest*, well, he just hit me and he got fifteen stacks that belong to me. You know how them young muthafuckas be wit' paper in their pocket for too long. Dig, take this number *555-905-7126.* "

"Alright, what's up?" I said after quickly jotting down the number.

"I need you to hit the nigga and collect that paper for me because I won't be back until Tuesday. Can you handle that for me?" he asked.

I hesitated before answering and finally after he called my name, I replied, "Yeah, I got you. Go ahead and breathe easy. Be safe, my nigga."

I called Na'feest, only 'cause I knew the nigga! I remember how we basically saved the nigga and put him on his feet. He was closer to J.O. than to me, but as far as I was concern he wasn't a threat at all.

He always showed me mad respect and he spoke to me

with admiration in his voice. He was a hustler to the heart! I agreed to go and pick him up because his baby's mom took his car. As I pulled up in front of the crib, he was standing there with his man *Ick-Rock*, another young muthafucka I basically introduced to the game.

He came towards the truck and they both got in. As we started to drive off, Na'feest said, "What's poppin', Ant Money?"

"What's poppin', homie?" I responded.

"J.O. don't be bullshitting about this money, do he?" Youngin asked me.

"You know how that go, business is priority."

"Well I got that for you anyway, fifteen stacks," he said with pride in his eyes, and continued, "Ant, I wanted to holla at you about something."

"What's good?" I asked sincerely.

"I been working for J.O. for a minute now and I always come through on time like I'm supposed to. He been promising to bless me so I could do my thing and that's all he been doing, *is promising*! I don't mind playing my part, but I'm trying to do some eating too! I been working the same spot for months now and I'm trying to come up. I know you can relate to wanting to get on."

"What does this shit have to do with me?" I asked.

"Everything! I don't know a lot of people in the position to help me, but I know you. I been stacking my paper the best that I can and I got thirty-five stacks in the bag. Fifteen for J.O. and twenty of my own! I don't wanna fuck wit' just anybody so I wanna know if you can set me out wit' a bird for twenty? Just this one time man. I got a spot and everything, but I ain't got no work and I respect you niggaz too much to go elsewhere for assistance."

"You trying to step ya game up, huh?" I asked with a smile.

"I need this Ant and I only got twenty joints, but yo, I'ma come back and when I do, I'm always gonna come correct. Me and Ick been waiting for a chance to get out the shadows. Can you help us?" Shorty was looking at me with all seriousness.

I wasn't trying to deal with this shit, but I remember wanting and I never liked the feeling. Besides, I played a part in these niggaz being in the game, so why should I deprive them of their chance to shine. Fuck it! I said, "I'm gonna do this shit for you this one time, nigga! You keep my name out of your business. I dig you, lil nigga, and I respect a hustler, but don't think for one minute that I'd hesitate to dig your graves. You dig me?" I explained firmly.

"Yeah! Yo, I got you and that's my word on everything."

"Say no more!" I concluded.

I had five bricks sitting at Kia's that I got stuck with and was in the process of getting out of there one way or another before the night was over and I just made a quick ten point five unexpectedly so I was doing myself a favor.

When we pulled up, Kia peeped out through the window and seeing that I wasn't alone, she didn't come and open the door. I walked to the door and punched in my security code. Once the light switched over, I escorted them into the living room and told them to hold tight for a minute and not to touch anything. I came back out two minutes later with a medical bag in hand that contained what they came for.

"Yo, Ick, clear that table right there," I said.

"Where you want me to put this stuff?" he asked.

"Just drop it on the floor so we can count this paper up and I can get you niggaz on your way."

Na'feest opened the book bag and began to lay the money out. We counted once, twice and a third time.

"Yo, I ain't counting this shit again. That's $34,500 so

you short five."

"Ick, I thought you had all this shit together? You fuckin' up man. Ant, I can get that five to you in the morning. It ain't about nothing," Na'feest said convincingly.

I was too tired to argue and besides the fact, I knew he was good for it. Stepping up to cop a brick, he better be or his run won't be long at all, so I reached down and opened the bag.

Na'feest spoke again..."That shit shaped like a football."

"Fuck what it's shaped like. You wanna weigh this shit up or what?" I said as I began to get irritated.

"I ain't even gonna put you through all that, Ant, I know what it's hitting for," Na'feest said excitedly.

"I'ma give you some advice, and you got a choice to accept it or reject it, but there ain't no charge, so I advise you to accept it. As much as I appreciate you being willing to take my word, business is always business! Never take a man's word when it comes down to business and always set personal feelings aside...and remember...,"

BONG! BONG!

Everything went black! I was thinking, but I couldn't see. I felt like I just got hit in my head with a bat. I was lying on the floor and I could hear the sound of feet shuffling around and I heard voices that sounded deep, real deep and slow like a record dragging. I knew I was shot!

"Yo, hurry up, nigga! Put that money back in the bag and get the medicine bag! Hurry up!"

I was still conscious and I couldn't believe these faggot ass nobody ass niggaz got me!

"You wanna check the crib out? I know this nigga holding."

"Fuck that shit! We gotta get the fuck outta here. Make sure that nigga dead."

I heard that as clear as day! I continued to lie there trying to hold my breathing. It was a no-win situation so I played dead, hoping the sight of me would be enough. Then I heard it again...*BONG*...then feet running!

When I got shot the first time, the first bullet grazed me behind the ear and my hand went up to cover it automatically and I guess it was out of reflex. The second bullet went through my shoulder. I laid on the ground with my hand and my forearm covering most of my head and the last bullet, shot out of fear most likely. Lodged inside my forearm....

I wanted to lay there and hope that it would be over soon, but something inside of me wouldn't let me. I yelled out for Kia. I don't think anything came out! Then, finally, I heard myself and so did she! I did what I could to raise up and I opened my eyes the best way I could as she stood there in front of me with tears in her eyes and both of her hands cupping her mouth from fear and shock. I reached for her and she extended her hands to help me onto my feet. She was screaming..."Oh, my God! What should I do?" Her body was trembling from fear.

I spoke to her and told her to get a towel to wrap my head. She ran and when she returned, I was leaning on the wall, holding my head. She wrapped the towel on my head and I grabbed her arm and said, "Listen to me, I need you to be calm. I need you to hear me! Grab the green duffel bag out the closet. You gotta get that work out the crib!" I waited and when she returned, I handed her my gun and my keys. "Put that shit in the hood of the car, the engine! Pull your truck up to the front of the house and get me to a hospital."

She placed her body under my arm and helped me to the front steps and while I waited, she took care of everything! As we drove to the hospital I told her, "We got robbed! The police are gonna question you. We got robbed! You were asleep and you woke up when you heard shots. Two Puerto

Ricans were running out when you came out. You were scared. They were tall! You don't know anything else. You hear me?...Do you hear me?"

"Yes! Yes! I hear you! Why is this happening? Baby, please don't die!"

"You call Big-Dee, tell him it was Na'feest and Ick-Rock if I don't make it." She pressed hard on the gas!

"Baby? Baby? Oh God, don't do this to me!"

The rest was a blur. I passed out eventually...I knew it was over....

On the fifth day...my eyes opened! Heavily sedated, the medication taking its full effect, I felt no pain! A nurse at my bedside was telling me to relax and to not get too excited as I attempted to move.

"Sir, do you know where you are?" she questioned.

I nodded my head and attempted to speak, but my mouth felt like I'd been chewing on sand. She reached toward the table and handed me a cup of water and assisted me with it. She repeated her question.

"In the hospital," I replied.

"Do you know why you're here?"

"Somebody...I got robbed...somebody shot me." I tried to raise up again, angry at the way I was violated and crossed up.

"Relax, sweetie, everything is alright now," she assured.

A doctor came into the room and explained to me how they saved my life after he checked my vital signs and for any type of discomfort.

He told me that I was denied visitors due to the extreme circumstances of my situation and that when a shooting victim is admitted and is unstable, a *code-word* or *phase* is used in order to determine who is and who is not a welcomed visitor for safety reasons and although people have been attempting to see me, they were not permitted. I understood, but I still would have appreciated waking up to see my baby girl, Victoria, sitting at my bedside, comforting me like they do in the movies.

"There are, however, a couple of detectives that would like to speak with you. Its procedure with this type of case," the doctor added.

"Yeah, I understand," I said.

He excused himself after telling me just how lucky I had been and that I should thank God every day for as long as I live!

A few moments later, not to my surprise, two detectives introduced themselves.

"Mr. Sands?...Mr. Jamir Sands?"

That was my alias and it would be tested for the first time.

"Yeah, what's up?" I snarled.

"I'm Detective Anderson and this is my partner, Detective Krowley with a K. We need to ask you a few questions if you're feeling up to it. Hopefully we can get through this as quickly and easily as possible. You know, for a minute, we didn't think we'd ever be able to question you, but somebody's on your side." The detective was pointing to the man upstairs.

"What you wanna know?" I asked innocently.

"First and foremost, what's your relation to a Miss La'Kia Smith?"

"She's a friend of mine...is she alright?"

"She's fine! So, bottom line, what happened on the night in question that would lead up to your being here in this condition?"

I told them a little bit of this and some of that, and nothing more, and after deciding that it was all bullshit, Detective *Krowley with a K* said, "Look, Mr. Sands, I know that you guys have a *code* or what have you and believe me when I tell you, we can relate, but if you're telling us that two unknown assailants just came to your friend's house and you just happened to be there and became a victim of a senseless crime, then either one of two things needs to happen."

"And what's that?" I asked sarcastically.

"One, maybe you should choose a new and safer profession or two, maybe I need to go find a doctor because if you think we would believe some nonsense like that, then you must not be in your right state of mind."

"Profession? What, you trying to imply something? I'm in my right state of mind and maybe you do need to find a doctor because I'm sitting here in the muthafuckin' hospital from bullets and telling you what the fuck happened and you got the nerve to tell me I'm lying and accuse me of selling drugs. Yeah, get a doctor, the best that money can buy...a psychiatrist...'cause you need some help. I answered your questions to the best of my knowledge and what you do and don't believe is irrelevant to me, so if you ain't here to charge me with anything, raise the fuck up, I got some healing to do!" I was heated!

"Gentlemen, gentlemen!" Detective Anderson said in an attempt to make me think he wasn't on either side. He continued..."Mr. Sands, we are not here to accuse you of anything. We simply want to help you and Miss Smith, and figure this whole situation out so that a man can be at a friend's house and not have to worry about dying! We are only doing our jobs. Here is my card. When you rest and begin to recuperate and if you feel that there's anything that...you know...just happened to slip your mind, please don't hesitate to call because believe it or not, we are on your side!"

With that, they left me to my thoughts and truthfully, I was afraid to be alone with them because my thoughts consisted of nothing but murder! There were no ifs, ands or buts about it. Those coward ass niggaz left me with no option. I once read *"Distrust any man in whom which the desire to punish is strong!"* Well, lying up in that bed, looking over myself...I didn't even trust myself....

After I was released, or signed myself out early, I contacted Victoria and told her to relax and that everything was alright and to pack some things because we were going on a trip for a few weeks. She had a thousand questions, combined with a million tears, and when I told her I would explain everything later, she got my point and I told her not to speak to anybody, under any circumstances, nobody!

I called the only person I felt I could trust and that was Big-Dee.

"Yo, nigga! Guess who's back?" I said reassuringly.

"Ant?" Big-Dee was surprised as hell to hear from me.

"You be knowing!"

"Yo, what the fuck is going on? Where you at?" he asked excitedly.

"Be easy, homie! Dig this. I want you to keep this conversation between the two of us. Don't nobody know I'm out so I'm gonna take a few weeks to get my mind right. Them niggaz tried to dead me, man! Yo, that shit was for real!"

"Them pussies is MIA. Don't nobody know nothing! The nigga J.O. put fifty stacks on them cats and you know it's a whole lot of niggaz trying to see that."

"Meet me at Kia's in a half, alright?"

"I'm on my way."

When the taxi pulled up, I had the driver circle the block twice before letting me out. When I walked in, Kia was all hugs, kisses and tears. She told me all about the detectives and I let her know she did a good job handling the beast. I explained that I was gonna be leaving for a while and surprisingly, she ain't put up no argument saying how she thought that was best for me and to be careful because they needed me. *They* being her and my unborn! She told me that she had taken the work to Dee and that he'd been calling every day trying to figure out what was going on with me. He'd been worried like crazy!...I smiled.

"I know, baby, I spoke to him and he's on his way. I'm leaving in a lil while. I just wanted to make sure that you got everything you need before I go."

"Don't worry about me! Do what you gotta do and get back soon and safe!...I know you taking her with you, but I ain't gonna start tripping, alright, baby?"

"We been through this shit before. Don't let no bullshit come between our understanding. Everything is gonna be everything, even better. You still with me?"

"Don't ask questions you already know the answer to! I love you too and if I gotta share you to keep you, I can wait it out."

Dee hit the door. I grabbed the few things I needed and we drove over to Victoria's. Along the way I told him my plans and every detail of what happened that day. As he listened, I could see the pain in his eyes! I told him that somebody would contact him and this month's work would be delivered to him and everything was to keep going as always. He asked what he should tell J.O. and I told him that I would take care of that. For now, just stay on everything and let me know if he hears anything about Na'feest and Ick-Rock.

"You sure Kia's alright with whatever?"

"That goes without saying. Yo, Ant, not for nothing...I prayed for you! I really did!"

"I know you did homie!" I smiled again.

I called Victoria to see if she was ready and to be out front with everything she needed in ten minutes. We pulled up to the curb and I didn't exit the car. Dee got out and told her to get inside while he placed her things in the back. When she got to the car, she opened the door and immediately began to cry from the sight of the bandages and I can only assume, from the sight of the side of my head! The swelling hadn't ceased and I definitely looked crazy. She placed her arms around me from the back seat and I touched her arms without any words being said.

"Where we headed to now?" Dee asked.

"To the airport! I got everything I need right here!" I said as I squeezed Victoria's arm tighter.

Dee said, "Man, if I had some liquor, we'd toast to that."

Before we went our separate ways I borrowed Dee's phone and dialed...*555-248-5276.*

The plane ride was relaxing and soothing! I attempted to ask the stewardess for some liquor and Victoria squeezed my hand so I changed my mind, or better yet, she did.

"Do you have any tea?" I asked.

"Yes, of course! Would you prefer any specific flavor, sir?" the stewardess asked cordially.

"Earl Grey." She once told me in a phone conversation it was her favorite.

Victoria smiled as she lifted her head from my shoulder and said, "You remembered."

I winked at her and said with a smile, "It's the small things that count, baby girl."

She smiled and nodded.

I almost felt at peace for the first time in a while. That is until she fell asleep, and as I watched her, thanking God for her being at my side, my conscious began to eat at me! My mind drifted as I thought about the fact that with everything that has happened, my incarceration, my being on the run, the drugs, the drama, my most recent, near death experience, Victoria was here through it all. I loved her! I wondered was it possible to love somebody and hurt them at the same time. This situation with Kia especially carrying my child was exactly that...*a situation* that got extremely out of hand! Six months pregnant! How was I gonna tell Victoria and not lose her? Maybe I was selfish, because I was dead wrong and I didn't deserve to have her, but something inside of me told me different. It was like, for all the bad that happened in my life, she was my one true reward! My oasis in the desert!

She looked so peaceful lying there with her head rested on my good shoulder. She was the epitome of what a good woman was and should be. At that moment, she was mine, so I forced myself to accept that reality and appreciate it while I could! I didn't want to lose her, but pain and pleasure really did co-exist. There never seemed to be pleasure without pain, in one form or another, but for now, I would seize the moment and accept it for what its worth! The world and all its treasures!

As we landed, she began to wake up and I told her, "We're here."

"Already?" she questioned looking out of the window.

"Yeah, baby, already," I said as I brushed the hair outta her face.

St. Tropez was the place we both agreed to have our honeymoon, and after what happened, *tomorrows* were hard to believe in, so I wanted to experience a honeymoon we might never have. At least that's how it seemed at that point in time. *"Live for the moment and seize the day!"* Trini was right about one thing! I had never seen with my own two eyes a place surrounded by so much beauty. I felt like a new man! I almost forgot for a while that this was only an escape from my life, which consisted of the harshest realities!

"What are you thinking about?" she asked.

"You!" I said in a matter of fact tone.

"What about me?"

"Well...,"

"I'm waiting."

"You look happy for once. I see you on the beach and its like you're free from the burden of misery and I don't want to have to get on a plane to give you that because you deserve it all the time." I paused. "And I'm thinking about getting out."

"What are you talking about?" she asked happily.

"You asked me on the day of X's funeral what it was I was trying to accomplish and what I felt I needed to prove, and truthfully, up until this moment, I really never knew! I want *this*! Not necessarily St. Tropez itself, but the peace of mind it offers, and it seems like it always costs to get what you want and I'm afraid to walk away because I'm good at what I do and I'm afraid to fail."

"Until you let it go, all this is gonna be nothing more than a vacation. I mean, baby, you're not exactly struggling financially and the world is filled with endless opportunities. Don't be afraid to have what you deserve. Besides the fact, you have the best thing in the world going for you already."

"And what would that be?" I asked wanting to really know.

"Me! And I have you and that, in my eyes, is a helluva start."

She smiled proudly and her smile said a thousand words.

"So?" she continued.

"So, what?"

"So, what are you gonna do?"

"I'm gonna...I'm gonna go get some ice cream!"

She looked confused as she said, "What does ice cream have to do with anything?"

That's what I get for sharing my thoughts! She was expecting an answer and I knew in my heart that she would-n't really want to hear the truth. The truth being that as much as I wanted to, it wasn't gonna happen...at least no time soon! So I said, "Ice cream has to do with today! There's no room for tomorrow until it gets here. Right now, I want to enjoy today! A little ice cream and a lot of you is what's gonna make that happen!"

She hit me in my chest playfully and said, "You think you're slick, don't you? Okay, we'll enjoy today and we'll talk about tomorrow real soon. How 'bout that, slickster?"

We spent the next hour enjoying our ice cream. The rest of the day and part of the night, we just spent enjoying one another, intimately, in so many ways.

Curiosity was getting the best of me, so finally, after eight days, I decided to call Dee and find out what he knew, and to plan for my return.

"Peace! What's good?" he said as he answered.

"You tell me! What's good, homie?"

"It's about time, damn nigga. You got a nigga on some worried shit! Yo, how you holding up? Is everything alright?" he asked concerned.

"Everything is good. It's between Tori and the sun, but yo, a nigga feeling damn near new. What's the latest? Did you get that work on time?"

"Man, did I? You dropped the bomb on a nigga. In the words of *K.R.S., "Moneys flowing, everything is fine."*

"So what's the word?"

"Ya man, J.O., tripping, feeling some type of way 'cause you ain't get at him before you left and them bitch ass niggaz are being stalked as we speak! I had ya peoples on them cats for two days now and you ain't call."

"Whoa! Breathe easy! Don't worry about J.O., I'ma handle that but yo, tell them niggaz to hold tight and keep doing what they doing. I'ma hit you from the airport on Thursday."

"Alright, family...one!"

"One."

I called J.O and he was definitely feeling some type of

way about me not calling him, so I explained to him that I thought it was best because the way shit had jumped off and I left because I didn't want any drama to come his way if them niggaz caught wind that I was alive. Besides, I instructed Dee to let him know my status, but not all the details.

"Come home, nigga," he said.

"I'll be there in a week, but yo, I want you to do me a favor. I appreciate the fact that you put that word for fifty in the streets, but I want you to dead that shit!"

"What! Man, I can't do that. Them muthafuckas was under my wing and that greedy shit don't sit right with me. They violated you and by doing that, them pussies violated me. Don't get soft on me, we in this together and, *I am my brother's keeper!*"

"Them niggaz ain't gonna show! At least not any time soon. They'll be back when they get the word that its sweet. Do what I asked you to do!"

"Yo, we'll rap when you get here, but alright! I'll do that. You sure you alright, nigga?"

"Most definitely!"

"See you when you touch down."

I didn't want him to know that I already had the drop on them niggaz and fifty stacks is a whole lot of answers to a whole lot of problems on the streets and I didn't want anybody to spoil what I was gonna do! I decided to stay a few more days, not that I wasn't eager to get home, but I wanted to look a hundred percent, even if physically I wasn't. I didn't want anybody to see me in a vulnerable state! Any signs of weakness would guarantee the vultures to circle!

Leaving was harder than I imagined it would be! Who wants to leave paradise? Victoria hadn't said much on the plane. I knew what she was thinking, and she was right! Things were about to change....

I decided to call J.O. from the airport and have him come get me instead of Dee, for political reasons. I didn't want to give him the impression that I was trying to distance myself from him and that I didn't trust him! Even though, *I was* and *I didn't.*

I had Dee come pick up Victoria and already explained to him why I was riding with J.O. and he told me that I was gambling, but evidently I knew what I was doing, so he handed me a burner and said to watch my back *and* my front! I told Victoria that everything was alright and that there was nothing to worry about.

For a second, it seemed like she was gonna start crying, but she smiled and gave me a hug and said, "I know baby...I know!"

For some reason, I knew she didn't mean it! She looked back at me the whole time while they drove off and it almost seemed like goodbye!

Fifteen minutes later, J.O. pulled up in his new Benz CL500 and once he spotted me, he got out and grabbed my bags.

"Damn! A nigga don't get a proper greeting no more?" I said.

"My bad, yo!"

He took my hand and pulled me toward him and hugged me and said, "I'm glad you're here."

We discussed a lot of things along the way and came to the conclusion that maybe I should play the back for a minute before I showed my face. When the time came to make my appearance felt *and* my return it would be as worthy of praise like *Jesus* and *Easter*! Everything would be alright as far as business was concerned.

I wanted to rock them young niggaz to sleep, so I kept tabs on them for the next two weeks. In the meantime, I spent most of my time between homes, with Victoria and

La'Kia. My daughter would be here in about two months and I had a lot of planning to do and a lot of decisions to make by then.

One thing for certain, my problems would be non-existent by then one way or another!

In the meantime, I was gonna get rich!

Chapter Seven
Connections

I was motivated, dedicated and determined to *be all I could be*, only *my* army consisted of lieutenants, runners, point men, workers and soldiers in the drug game! We were at war with the police, Feds, D.E.A., A.T.F. and muthafuckin' snitches, but most importantly with time, because it definitely waited for no man and according to the laws of gravity, *what goes up, must come down* and I knew in my heart it was only a matter of *time*, so I made a promise to myself that I would go above and beyond the call of duty to bring this war to a sensible, profitable and peaceful end before it got too late, but only God knew when that would be....

Truthfully, I never even dreamed that things would ever be this good financially, but they were and I wasn't in a position to be doing no complaining. For the first time in my life, time was on my side and everything just seemed to fall in place!

Today was *my* muthafuckin' day! I felt like a star in my own right! As I drove around the city, it felt as if everyone just paused for a moment to stop and stare and acknowledge my presence and at the time, I didn't even care if it was a good or bad thing! I was that nigga!

I began my day early that morning making my rounds to the best lawyers that money could buy in order to begin the appeal process for my homies. Ant-Live, Y.T, Ani-Dog and I paid in full, with certain financial promises for any good news! *Good news* being time reduced or freedom! This was theirs too! They needed to know this, and I did everything within my power to let them know this! Even though Double-M refused, saying it was useless, I blessed him too!

After I wrapped everything up with the attorneys, I got a call from Big-Dee telling me that things were going a little faster than we planned this month and the work was getting low, but the money was coming like crazy and that I might wanna think about investing in a *Scrooge McDuck* type vault.

"You comical ass nigga!" I said.

"Yeah, but truth is truth, homie, and you exactly that! The truth manifested in the flesh," he said as he gave me that funny ass laugh.

"Yo, we gotta get up later on and do something to break up the monotony of this routine shit! Dig me? Between now and then, be safe out here, my nigga, and get my mutha-fuckin' paper stacking, nigga."

I laughed and he responded, "Yeah, aiight massa' Boss Man" in his best impression of a slave doing a lil jeffing!

I had some real important business to attend to and I woke up out of my sleep that morning thinking of nothing else. I had somewhere to be!

Three hours later, I found myself on the highway in a silver Dodge Intrepid that I had rented from an old friend who was down on his luck, or better yet, down on his *bucks*.

As I entered the town, I hit the back roads until I reached my destination. The building was some shit straight out of a horror flick, but perfect for what was to come! I parked about thirteen blocks away near the baseball stadium where a vehicle with out of town plates wasn't a conspicuous thing and decided it would be best to take a thirteen block walk. As I walked, I thought about how I bumped heads with these two young niggaz I was on my way to meet! *I was out of town at a club, doing it up real big and found myself way out of character, alone in a strange place, chasing after this bad ass Dominican broad, allowing the liquor and that Hydro to consume me! I had left the club early and went to my "Range" so I could have first dibs on some parking lot pimping, and as shorty exited the club, there I was, right in her view letting her know that she was chosen by a "Boss" for the night. She saw me and walked right past where I was standing and jumped right inside the passenger seat of my "Range" and looked at me as if to say, "Are you coming?" I liked shorty already! When I got in, I asked her, "Where we headed to, ma?" and she said, "I watched you undressing me all night with your eyes, so now we're gonna see if you're really up to the job! I don't frequent no telly's, so the choice is yours!...Your place or mines?"*

She knew damn well I wasn't from there so there wasn't much of an option! We headed to *her place* and as we entered the crib, I was disappointed immediately and not even surprised when I noticed two niggaz sitting on the couch, guns in hand! They had the drop on me and I didn't wanna do any running because the odds were already against me. *Damn! This funky bitch set me the fuck up, and I let it go down too! What the fuck was I thinking about?* At least that was the impression I was under, up until the taller of the two began to speak.

"Ay, my man, go on and breath easy! You just followed the wrong bitch home. Give us a minute and you can go ahead and roll, aiight?"

He eased his gun away from my direction and pointed it towards the broad and said, "You! On the other hand, you might not be so lucky!"

I looked at shorty and she acted as if she expected this and looked at me and said, "Maybe next time, Papi," and because I wasn't really hip to the situation at hand, I ain't do no responding!

The shorter of the two grabbed the broad up, placed handcuffs on her and threw her onto the couch! I was thinking *police*, but as they began to place duct tape around her mouth, all my ideas went out the door, so I had no choice but to *breath easy* and hope to make it out the way I made it in! The initial sight of the burners basically stripped me of my high and I was glad about that because I needed to be 100 percent prepared mentally for what I may not have been in a position to do physically!

They sat down on either side of shorty, who by now was just sitting there motionless with beautiful sensual, seductive, pleading eyes! *Damn! She was sexy as hell*, but now was definitely not the time for lusting! I spoke in a calm and clear voice as I said, "Dig this here. Like you said my man, evidently, I definitely followed the wrong bitch home, and this problem right here ain't none of mines...ya feel me?" I waited for a response from the taller cat because he seemed to be in charge of whatever it was that was in progress and besides all that, I did remember him saying something about letting a nigga go!

"Yeah, I feel you playa' but *dig this*!" The shorter one said with a great deal of emphasis on *Dig This* as he continued..."You seem to have misinterpreted this whole scenario right here. This," he said pointing his gun towards shorty, "is anything *but* our problem. She's our *business*, nothing more, nothing less! You being here like this was unexpected, so now, your presence has become a problem! Our *only* problem! It's unfortunate because problems are either solved or eliminated and you don't seem to be one of these *in the way ass muthafuckas* out here, but I don't see no solution to this problem without having to eliminate you! Ya feel me?"

What the fuck was I thinking about leaving my burner in the truck? Damn! Where the fuck is the candid camera? Somebody tell me this is a joke and it ain't about to go down like this, I thought, as I leaned forward in my seat and looked this cat straight in the eye and said, "If all this is about some foul business or whateva', cool! I can respect that, but it ain't no profit one way or another in y'all trying to do me dirty! Like I said, I don't know this broad like that; or at all for that matter. You can let me raise up and whatever's going down never happened."

The taller of the two finally spoke up. "What's your name, family?"

I knew that if I kept talking that my chances were gonna get better so I lied and said *Jahaad.*

"Is that right? *Jahaad.*" He said my name as if he admired the sound of it or something. "Well, *Jahaad*, relax, and let me run a situation by you. After we get through that, then maybe we can all find some common ground and come to some type of understanding." Smiling, he continued, "That is, if you're not too busy."

"Not at all," I responded trying to maintain my composure.

"I dig this nigga right here, no bullshit. He playin' his hand and he ain't even looked at the cards yet!" the shorter of the two said searching for a response from his man. He didn't receive one because he was deep in thought. He reached into his coat, pulled out a blue steeled .38, emptied all of the bullets into his other hand, slowly placed one of them back into the cylinder and placed the gun in front of me. I didn't know what the fuck was about to go down!

He said, "Now, here's the situation! I do what I do for a

living, but one of my vices is the fact that I'm an impulsive gambler."

I searched his eyes for the answer to this riddle, but I came up empty as he continued.

"This bitch right here ain't gonna see another day regardless of what happens! Like he said, she's business and that deal was closed way before tonight! Now, I'm willing to bet that you're as sharp as you look and when time comes, you'll make the wisest choice."

They both sat there, guns pointed in my direction and told me to place the gun on my lap. "Go 'head, take it." I hesitated and the taller one continued, "Playa', I'm a man of my word. Anything that happens to you is gonna be *your choice* completely, but know this here, there's one bullet in that gun. If, and I mean *If* you choose to use it, make the next choice ya best choice!"

I reached out for the gun slowly, never once taking my eyes off of these two cats, and when my hand touched the cold steel, I felt weak for a moment as though everything was coming to an end, right then and there. Fortunately that wasn't the case. I eased back up almost as slowly as I bent down and placed the gun in my lap! I asked them, "Now what?"

The taller cat continued again. "Now! Since you don't know this bitch and have no idea what's going on, I'm gonna get you better acquainted with her and bring you up to speed. Then, you have a decision to make, aiight?"

"*Jahaad*, I want you to meet *Lissette*. Truly one of the baddest bitches out here in more ways than one. You see, Lissette is neither a friend or foe to me and my man here, as I said *business* and what I mean by that is, I guess you could say an associate of ours just happened to be married to her, not through the courts, but through the *Game*. Being as though *Lissette* here played the role of *Wifey*, she had access to details of his lifestyle and business, which, if you ask me, was foolish on his part, but I'm paid to work, not to judge. Now, unfortunately, the powers that be have him in a fucked up predicament at the moment and he's facing more time than we can count on all of our fingers and toes together. Fortunately, there's a way to see light in a dark situation and the only thing that prevents that light from being seen is *Lissette* here," he said as he looked from me to her with hate in his eyes. He didn't even have to say any more because I knew what it was hitting for!

"She's the key to everything. The Feds seem to think this bitch's voice box is worth a great deal and she's appeared once so far, and before this record contract is signed and the ink dries, allowing this bitch to go *Platinum*, our services were paid for and that brings us up to the present! Now, my line of work is strictly for business purposes and you were right when you said that *there was no profit in doing you dirty*, so I ask myself, *where is the profit in letting you go?* I dig the way you handlin' yourself and I can clearly see that you's a real nigga and I consider myself a great judge of character, so how can we get through this where everybody will be happy? How does that saying go? *One hand washes the other and in turn, they both wash the face.* Yeah! That's it! So what can you do for me and my man that would warrant you getting up outta here?"

I thought about my answer and weighed my options, two niggaz, two burners, two clips, one *in the way ass bitch*, and me with one bullet.

The shorter of the two broke the silence and said, "Well, playa', what's on your mind?"

I grabbed the gun off of my lap and neither of them even blinked. Without hesitation, I pointed the gun in their direction and...*BOOM*...as I placed the gun back on the table, carefully, Lissette's eyes watered as the blood eased its way out of her chest!

"That's what the fuck I'm talkin' 'bout. I knew you was a real nigga," the taller cat said as he cocked his gun back, and BOOM, BOOM, finished what I started!

I didn't shoot her because she was a "*fuckin' rat,*"' cause for all I know, it was *their* story and besides the fact, how could I do that if I wasn't willing to travel the world and get at everybody that I knew that was on that type of time! Fuck that! I pulled the trigger because my life just happened to be that much more valuable than hers! It wasn't the first time and at the pace I was going, I highly doubt it would be the last! Not knowing her just made it much more easier, or at least that's what it seemed. I calmly said, "Now what?"

The taller one said, "Now, we get the fuck away from all this. Follow me! Grab that ratchet and come on."

I did exactly that because my prints were definitely on it and I was glad he remembered because I wasn't thinking about it. As I was leaving out, I took one last glance at Lissette and thought to myself, *It's a shame but it looks like there won't be a next time, mami!*

We got out and somehow we all ended up in my Range. I pulled off with the lights off, and after a few blocks I was instructed to hit the lights. Naturally, I complied! We drove in complete silence for what seemed like an eternity until the shorter of the two spoke.

"Jahaad, that was some icy ass shit."

The taller of the two said, "No bullshit, that was some real shit and I'ma keep it funky with you on the strength of that." As he looked around the truck, he said, "From the looks of things, you definitely seem to be about your business in more ways than one and I respect a real nigga. We ain't holding you hostage or no shit like that. You played your part and we played ours the best we could, and given the circumstances, I think everything worked out for the best. I know you ain't expect shit to jump off like it did tonight, but for what it's worth, it wasn't personal at all and game recognized game, so hopefully you ain't feeling no type of way about this shit."

Truthfully, I wasn't! I was *feeling* the way these niggaz carried themselves. I needed niggaz like that on my team to keep things in order. Yeah, it was a hectic night, but I saw potential in this whole situation. The only problem was, how could I convince these niggaz of that and capitalize? Fate is when two or more people meet under the most extreme or unordinary circumstances and this fell under those categories so it had to be just that...so I said, "Like you said, *Game Recognize Game* and I ain't in a position to knock another man's hustle, 'cause I wouldn't want a nigga to knock mine, and I believe it wasn't personal because maybe under the same circumstances, if our roles were reversed, I would have done the same because it was the smartest move. I ain't no gambling type muthafucka' but evidently you're a good judge of character. As a matter of fact, a great judge of character! Self preservation is common law in this game and I, unlike most niggaz, respect and acknowledge the rules of the game."

"Gangsta!" the shorter of the two said, with a smile on his face. "Pull up right here, homie," he said as he pointed to the right side of what seemed like nowhere!

I figured this is where we would part company and I had to say something, so I spoke my mind. "Dig right, not for nothing I appreciate you standing true to your word and all that and believe me, that's what's up, and I might be pushing my luck but the way I see it, *a closed mouth don't get fed*, so hypothetically speaking, if a muthafucka was interested in contacting you cats, strictly for *business* purposes, how would he go about doing that because I personally know a place where your services, *so to speak*, would be in high demand and most definitely appreciated *and* profitable!"

I waited for a response as I glanced down at my watch for the first time that night. *5:32 a.m. Damn! It's definitely been a long night!* I thought.

"Is that right?" asked the taller of the two.

"Yeah, without a doubt!" I responded.

"How do *you* profit in all this?"

"Hypothetically speaking, I'd be the one doing all the hiring, dig me?"

"Why? I mean, it's obvious that you're built to handle your own business affairs, so why you wanna waste good money like that?"

"It's like this here. I spend my time trying to make and break a dollar and there's no such thing as wasting money if its spent wisely, and excluding placing myself in fucked up situations like tonight, I pride myself in fucked up situations like tonight, I pride myself on my ability to make wise decisions! It's not a question of what I can and can't handle. It's about what's best for me and what it is I'm trying to accomplish. You feel me? And besides the point, what happened tonight didn't just happen for no reason! The average joker might find the fact that we even sitting here conversating like this to be crazy, but I ain't him and all I know is everything happens for a reason and I see opportunity! You may not fully understand that, but I'm in a position to make a lot of good days *better*! Like you said earlier, *one hand washes the other and in turn, they both wash the face.* After tonight, the trust factor should be self evident, I mean, we can walk away from this shit and just like that, it never happened, but I feel that would be a waste so what's really good?"

"*555-248-5276* is what's really good."

"That's what I'm talking 'bout," I said as I reached for my phone to place the number in its memory and asked,

"Who am I asking for?"

The shorter of the two turned to me and said, "The other hand."

"Right! I feel you," I said.

Before we parted and went our separate ways, they turned back towards me and said that as an act of good faith, the first ones on them!...Of course, I held them to it! But that's another story.

"Yo, I'm a block away! I'ma come through the back!"

"It's about time, nigga! I was beginning to wonder."

"I'll explain all that when I come through," I said to the taller half of *the other hand*.

As I entered the back of the building, which evidently once upon a time served its purpose as a means for somebody's shelter, I began to second guess the ill intent that was consuming me. *"They just kids,"* I heard somebody say or something, but just as quickly as it came, it went!

"How you brothers feeling?" I asked.

"Man! You know how that go. A muthafucka can't do too much of all that, especially in this line of work, but for what it's worth, we ready when you ready. This your show!"

"Where them niggaz at?" I asked.

Them niggaz being *Na'Feest* and *Ick-Rock*. When we caught wind of where them niggaz were, my first instinct was to let my people do what it is they do, but my pride wouldn't allow it to go down like that! They acted without thinking and now here they were sitting on my coke with no way to get rid of it because all they knew was the city, and fifty thousand reasons prevented them from going home. The city belonged to me and they were no longer welcomed visitors!

I had my peoples, who were getting bored with just keeping an eye on these faggots, do what they could to cut into them and they did exactly that! Within two days, Na'Feest opened the door and let them know that they had some coke to put out on the market, and with money in hand, my people attempted to cop something light just for the sake of keeping them comfortable and asleep, but Ick-Rock and Na'Feest told them that they wasn't trying to be out there like that, but they would sell them a brick for twenty-four and if they was feeling it like that, they would come back through with all the work they needed!

I had to admit that it was the smartest move, because they really didn't know these cats and at the same time, they probably weren't trying to do a whole lot of traveling with the coke on hand, but they were desperate to get rid of it and the promise of *all the work they needed* would hold a stick up off till a better day.

I told my people to tell them that they wasn't built for all that, at least not at once, but they know a few hustlers who would bite for twenty-six and if they could make that happen, could they see some type of PC! Of course they agreed to it and I just happened to be the gullible hustler copping for twenty-six! Only they had no idea what was about to go down! I anticipated the moment when our eyes would first meet because as far as these niggaz knew, I was dead!

I let my people enter the room first so that they would be at ease by the time I decided to pop my head in. I saw them before they saw me and with my guns already in my hands, I spoke up. "Long time no see fellas."

The look on their faces could only be described as a *Kodak moment*. Before either of them could react and try to reach, my people had their burners cocked back and pointed in their direction. The element of surprise is a muthafucka, and I had the drop on these coward ass niggaz! The shorter part of my team frisked them and found that only Ick-Rock was holding a .380 in his jacket pocket.

"Go ahead and have a seat! Don't you niggas know guns

are bad? They cause pussies and cowards to get hearts and..."

I was interrupted by Na'Feest pleading, "Ant! Listen to me man, it wasn't suppose to go down like that!"

"SHUT THE FUCK UP! You better not part your lips to say another muthafuckin' word...you hear me, muthafucka?"

He began to say something, but after looking in my eyes and seeing what had to be the devil, he simply shook his head in agreement.

"Yeah, lil nigga! I'm hip that it wasn't supposed to go down like that. I wasn't supposed to make it, but I did and now somebody gotta be held accountable for this," I said as I moved my ear with my finger to expose the scar from the first shot. Tears were in Na'Feest's eyes and I didn't feel anything for him! I looked over to Ick-Rock who just sat there and followed me with his eyes.

"Tie these niggaz to them chairs and make 'em face each other. You niggaz crossed me up about some change! *Some change!* You could've talked me outta that...make sure them joints tight," I said as I interrupted myself for a second.

"Yeah! They cool! They ain't going nowhere."

I put my burner on the table and reached into my pocket and pulled out a straight razor. I stood behind Na'Feest and used my left hand to cup his chin as I eased the razor round to the front of his neck. I looked straight across to Ick-Rock as I began to speak. "We gon' play a game called who wants to make it out of here with just a scar as a reminder, and before you get to thinking that's a bad thing, the loser's dead! So, tell me what's on your mind."

Na'Feest, with tears rolling down his face, was the first to break as he tried to look up at me. "I was only gonna pay you fifteen and ask you to help me. That's all I wanted! I swear to God, yo! Ick wanted to rob you and Ant, I kept telling him no! I told you that, didn't I?" He was referring to his homie sitting across from him and continued." He told me we was gonna come up, and that nobody was gonna get hurt and as long as we just disappeared with the money, everything would work out. I didn't know it was gonna go down like that, you gotta believe me, Ant."

"Nigga, I ain't *GOT* to do shit! Stop fuckin' crying! You wasn't crying when you was taking my fuckin' paper so shut the *FUCK UP!*" I looked back over to Ick-Rock and still no emotion. "Is that what happened, nigga?"

He just stared at me and I swear for one brief second, I respected the lil niggaz' heart! That is until the moment when my grip got tighter on Na'Feest and the razor split his neck open from one side to the other. Blood squirted across Ick-Rock's face, his shirt and his eyes and not once did I blink as I said, "This is for being a fuckin' rat and for being such a fuckin' coward."

Ick-Rock started squirming around in his chair, shaking his head not believing what he just saw.

"That's how you kill a muthafucka! You hear me? That's how you handle ya fuckin' business, nigga! I ain't gonna cut you, so go ahead and relax yourself."

I put the razor back into my pocket after wiping it clean on Na'Feest's jacket. I didn't think he'd mind too much!

Ick finally spoke up. "Ant, I know I fucked up and I wish it never happened, but I couldn't get no help! Niggaz wasn't trying to see me out there! I was starving!"

"Don't think this is one of them dumb ass movie scenes where you talk your way outta what's coming! Nigga, I don't give a mad ass fuck about you starving! Fuck I look like, a soup kitchen? You chose to play the gangsta' role, so play it all the way to the end."

I grabbed my burner off of the table and looked him directly in his eyes and he screamed my name, *ANT,* in one last attempt to plea for his life, but it wasn't good enough, so I squeezed the trigger something like eight or nine times into his face. I was violated by these niggaz in the worst way, and I heard that voice again..."*They only kids.*"

I wrestled with my conscience, and I almost lost! Yeah! They were kids, playing a grown up game and I know I've done my share of dirt in my life, but I was always prepared, at least to some extent, to deal with the consequences of my actions and maybe that shit was extreme, but damn, they tried to dead me over some punk ass shit! They were in the fuckin' way anyway and I did them a favor by not prolonging the inevitable. Damn! I felt fucked up, almost like *Scarface...*"*Why you make me do that, Manny,*"...only I never considered them to be friends, but just the same, I knew them. I knew they people too...Man, fuck all that, they knew me and they knew my people too and that ain't stop them from doing what they did, so, fuck them niggaz!

This wasn't the first time and, unfortunately, I knew it wouldn't be the last, but for some reason, this shit just seemed to bother me...I'm slippin'.

"Hello," my cell phone caught me off guard.

"Yo! Ant! Where you at?" Big-Dee screamed in my ear.

"Fuck you mean, where I'm at? Where I be nigga! When we start screaming locations on the phone?" I screamed back.

I ain't mean to get out on my man like that, but for the past few days, I wasn't in my right state of mind and I was paranoid about the events that took place a few days ago.

Big-Dee said, "You alright, nigga?"

"Yeah, nigga, I'm good. My bad! Nigga just got some things on his mind, you feel me?"

"I hear you! But yo, dig this here. I think you should go holla at ya peoples, man, 'cause shorty just hit my phone talking 'bout she got a message on the machine from ya wifey and I don't know the details, but I guess she was poppin' it real gangsta like to Kia, and man...,"

I cut him off thinking to myself that I didn't need no extra soap opera shit right now.

"Did Kia say she spoke to her?" I asked.

"Nah, but she said she been trying to hit you all day and you ain't been answering so she called me, I guess hoping you would be with me or whatever."

I started laughing, 'cause some things you can't do nothing but laugh about.

"Yo, what's so funny?" Big-Dee asked me.

"I just can't picture Tori coming at shorty on no aggressive shit and I damn sure can't picture Kia being on no shook time. This shit is crazy, but it ain't nothing a nigga can't handle!"

"I'ma get up wit' you later on. I'm taking wifey up to the city to cop some clothes and what not for my babies so I should be back around eleven tonight, so make sure you hit me and let me know what's good. If I shoot through my sister's spot, you want me to holla?"

"Yeah! Tell her I said...Have car, will travel."

"I'ma do exactly that. One."

"One."

I thought about taking that trip myself, but the truth is I faced too many adversities to run away from a situation that I knew I had to deal with. I don't know how the fuck Tori got that info, but then again, I been doing too many things at once and the drama been non-stop so why should I expect otherwise. Life is hectic! I knew I was gonna have to deal with this shit sooner or later but honestly, sometimes the truth just ain't worth the consequences.

I was glad that the situation between me and Kia was understood. Then again, that was wishful thinking and *illlogic* because once you allow a woman to get close enough to you to start catching feelings, all that *understanding* shit goes out the door. And here she was pregnant, carrying my seed and a lot more feelings and emotions than was agreed upon, so I can't really blame her, but I can't force myself to love someone! Not that she wasn't worthy of that, but my heart was completely with Victoria and my life would feel incomplete without her...Damn! I fucked up!

I went to the bar down on the block and hoped that if I surrounded myself with muthafuckas who had way more problems than me, I could ease the pain of the possible out-come of my reality, which ultimately would end in losing what I thought meant more to me than anything...Victoria.

I sat at the bar talking to Yvette about how no matter what changes, the bar always remained the same and about her father's appeal. Her father being the first that I ever knew of personally who got indicted on that RICO bullshit back in the day. Now I knew why he didn't complain too much about when we used to rush his bodega and steal mad shit. I guess he could afford it, but one thing for certain, you would have never guessed it from appearances! Yvette used to be my sweetheart back in the day, but time definitely took its toll on her. She was still attractive...Puerto Rican, blond hair, green eyes, thick in all the right places..., but she just lost that sex appeal she once had. Working a bar all day wasn't too healthy for anyone and I think she just talked too much now because of it.

"You know my father still asks about you? I guess it's safe to say he thinks you were good for me, huh?" she said.

"Is that right? Well tell him I said what's good and that his little girl was afraid to become a woman before her time."

She slapped my hand as she said, "You holding that against me after all these years? Lucky for me because you turned out to be doggish like the rest of them."

I know that's right, but I know she wished she would have came up off that ass back then when a nigga was type pressed.

My aunt Gina came into the bar and immediately spotted me. Yvette smiled that *fuck you* smile knowing I wasn't trying to be bothered by my aunt. I was trying to get twisted!

"Nephew, oooh, there go my baby," she said drunk as hell or high. I really couldn't tell the difference any more. Not that I ever really could. She hugged me and I hit her with that homie hug. One arm, one elbow to keep the distance.

"What's going on, Gina? How are you?" I replied.

"Ant, my baby, fine as hell. Boy I swear if you wasn't my family, I'd have been saved you from all these scandalous ass bitches out here, 'cause you know ain't none of 'em no good! You know that, don't you, baby?"

The question and the statement were directed to Yvette, and she rolled her eyes and walked away when I smiled. Comedy was definitely my aunt's forte.

"You want something to drink?" I asked, already knowing.

"If you buying, I don't wanna be rude and turn you down. So what brought you down here to be wit' us common folk?"

"A yo, Yvette, let me get two shots of Remy." She rolled her eyes again.

"What you mean 'common folk'? Since when I ain't been welcome in my hood?" I felt a lil offended.

"Ain't nobody say you wasn't welcomed, you just doing a lot of things now a days. I hear things and I see like everybody else and it ain't nothing wrong with not coming 'round here if you ain't got to, shit, let me get me some money and one of them big ol' cars you got and these poor muthafuckas wouldn't ever see auntie Gina 'round here no more. And that's the truth!"

"I hear you, Auntie," I smiled.

My family was anything but family and I never heard from anybody other than my sister, unless they wanted something because other than that, they always had some dumb shit to say about me, but I ain't worry about it too much 'cause some people were just set in their ways.

"Baby, I gotta get up outta here. You think you can give your ol' auntie a ride across the bridge? Or if you busy, I could catch a cab, but I ain't really hit that number yet, so I'm..."

I knew it was coming so I cut her off and said, "I'm waiting here to meet somebody, but here," I reached into my pocket and gave her fifty dollars.

She snatched the money like I was playing or something and took her last shot. Before she could even get it all down, she kissed me all wet on my cheek and said, "See, now that's why you my favorite nephew and I'm your favorite auntie."

I shook my head as she worked her way to the front door. I knew two things for certain. One, wasn't none of that money going on no cab and two, all of it was coming right back to me because she was on her way down the block to cop something off one of my workers. She really did *use* to be my favorite aunt!

This crack game was like a volcano that erupted! They could set up barriers and do everything in their power to attempt to control or stop it, but it was too powerful to be controlled or stopped. Shit, they couldn't even really slow it down if they wanted to and they tried every fuckin' day!

I talked with Yvette for a little while and she told me a bunch of drama about her baby father getting locked up and how she was struggling trying to run the bar and push a little bit of weed on the side. Like everybody else, she was pressed for some paper, so I did the best that I was willing to do and copped a quarter of that good green and found my way to the door.

After half-listening to Yvette, I decided to call Kia and get the process started. She answered on the first ring like she was anticipating a call.

"Stop fucking calling here."

"Who the fuck is you talking to like that?" I bellowed.

"Ant, I didn't know it was you! Your fuckin' girl keeps calling here every five minutes saying she got the number and she's gonna get the address and...Ant, why haven't you been answering your phone?"

"I thought I lost that shit, but I left it in the front of my young boy's car this morning and he just got that shit to me and all my messages is full. So what's all this shit about Tori and you?"

"Oh! So you just happen to lose your phone. Convenient!"

I snapped. "You can save that sarcastic shit for a sucka! Who the fuck is *you* to lie to. I ain't in no type of mood to hear no bullshit so dig yourself, alright!"

"Alright! Damn! Are you coming over 'cause we gotta talk?"

"I'm on my way, but yo, I ain't trying to come through that door to hear no bullshit, so if we gon' be on some kiddie time, let me know now...." I might have been wrong for snapping on her because it wasn't *her* fault, but at the same time, she knew what this whole thing was hitting for from jump street, so it was her choice to get her feelings involved so none of this should be a surprise!

"I just wanna talk to you, that's all," she said.

"Ten minutes, and yo, take the ringer off."

"Alright."

I wasn't too worried about Kia and the position she would play because she wasn't going anywhere. Yeah, she pushed that love issue but when it all came down to it, she was still the same broad who was quick to choose status and position above all else! Victoria, on the other hand, was everything that *she* was not and I felt bad because in my heart, I would give everything up at the drop of a dime to make this right, but in my mind, I knew I wasn't willing to and I couldn't and it was a shame because I knew it and didn't have the strength and self-control to just walk away. This life was a part of me! I lived and breathed this shit and now here I was at the crossroad and I was willing to choose pain and stress and all the madness that created this *game* over nothing but pleasure, because when a woman loves you and it's so real that you can feel that shit physically, there's nothing that can compare to it...nothing!

My phone was vibrating as I made my way towards Kia's and when I checked the number I found myself afraid to actually answer my phone...it was Victoria and I was feeling that liquor already and just like that, it was gone. I answered the phone with crazy hesitation....

"Yo, what's good?" I said calmly. I already knew the answer, but fuck it.

"From the looks of things, *you* seem to be," she replied.

I already knew where this was headed, but I dummied up and said, "What's that suppose to mean?"

"Listen, *Ant, Anthony* or whatever the hell you're calling yourself today, I know you know exactly what the hell that means, so all the games you call yourself playing stop now! We need to talk."

What could I say? She was right so as I made a U-turn and changed my course, now heading to Tori's, I said, "I'm on my way, alright?"

"If you plan to come here with anything but the truth, don't even bother to waste your time 'cause I can't deal with this shit! Why! How could you do this to me? How could you do this to us?" She started crying and I felt that shit, literally! I felt her pain and to know I was the cause of it was eating me up inside. I was at a loss for words because all my emotions were balled up in a knot in my chest and throat, but my mind and thoughts were racing so fast that I couldn't open my mouth in time to get the right combination of words out. By the time I attempted to respond to my baby girl, it was something like, "I'm coming," or some stupid ass shit and...it was too late, because I was speaking to a dial tone!

I was contemplating turning the fuck around because this was something I really wasn't prepared for...at least not on an emotional level. Yeah, I've been known to pop that good shit and run that good game in my life, but this wasn't one of those cases. This was the woman who taught me how to love and to accept it in return. The woman who I planned to one day marry. The woman who I thought I was doing all this for. This was the woman I loved, sincerely and deeply! This was my future! Games wouldn't do!

I stretched a twenty-minute drive into a good forty-five minutes thinking of what to say and how to say it and the only thing I could come up with was the truth! She was worthy of that.

When I got there, I almost turned back around when I saw her sister's car in the driveway. This broad was on an *anti* Ant campaign and this situation was all the more reason for her to win.

I caught myself before I rang the doorbell thinking, *Damn, why the fuck do I feel like a stranger in my own crib?* And as I put my key in the hole, the door swung open.

"What's going on, Shay? Where's Tori?" I asked her sister as she stared at me with a smile on her face.

"Let me ask you something before you go in there. You always claiming that you love my lil sister, so why would you go out of your way to prove otherwise? I mean...me...I knew you was a dog, but she don't deserve this shit. I..."

I cut her off 'cause I wasn't trying to hear that nut ass shit.

"Yo! Get your shit and raise up! Me and her will deal with whatever, but you need to mind ya business and speed the fuck on and that was the first and last time I'm gonna ask you!" I said.

I think she was about to respond when Victoria appeared in the doorway and dramatic would be an understatement! She looked as if she just got news that her mother passed or something. Like she had been crying forever. She looked helpless and I wanted to reach out to her and assure her that I was there and everything would be alright...but just as fast, I realized that her mother didn't pass and I was the cause of this, so I highly doubted that this would be one of those forgiving television scenes where we would embrace and all the other bullshit!

She broke the silence and said, "It's okay, Shay, I can handle this."

Shay gave me a look, a sisterly warning, and then without word, she opened the door all the way and stepped to the side, inviting me into my own home!

"You know, it's funny how I feel right now. I mean, I feel hurt and disappointed and something else that I can't really describe, but I'm not mad at you and I don't hate you. I'm mad at myself. I knew this..."

I cut her off and attempted to speak and she looked me in my eyes for the very first time and said, "No, please, let me say what I need to say because if I don't, it won't get said. Can I have that much or is this really all about *Anthony* and what he says and wants?"

"You right! I'm listening," I responded.

"Like I said, I knew this was coming and so did everybody else, but I refused to deny myself the possibility that me and *everybody else* could be wrong. I had to know because I believed that if I played my part to the fullest, that I could somehow make this work and you would choose *me* and *us* above all else, and here I am crying and hurting so I guess *I* was wrong!" She was laughing through her sobs and tears, but there was no joy in that laughter at all.

I fucked up! "Baby, listen to me. I made a fucked up choice and you have every right to feel the way you do. I'm not gonna sit here and say I'm sorry because it would be like a slap in the face and you deserve more than to hear me say that. I would give anything to make this right, not for me, or everybody else, but for you! You're about the only thing that I have, or had, that means anything and everything to me and I thought of so many ways to tell you, but I was selfish because I didn't wanna lose you and I still don't!"

She stood there in silence, so I continued...

"I've experienced so many things with you, Tori, feelings that I didn't believe existed or didn't believe I was capable of feeling. That broad don't mean nothing to me! I made a mistake that I couldn't correct and I'm not trying to make myself sound all innocent and shit, 'cause I'm responsible for her being pregnant, but I can't deny my seed because I was a foolish muthafucka, but don't none of that change the way I feel about you! You can believe what you want, but you can't deny me *my* feelings. All this right here is for you," I said as I pointed around the house.

"I rearranged my whole fucking life for you, Anthony, everything! Do you think this matters to me? Do you think any of this...this shit means anything to me?" She began taking off her jewelry and said, "I didn't want none of this! I didn't need none of this! No! You! You wanted this!"

As she walked away towards the bedroom, she repeated what she said. When she returned, she had her car keys and a bunch of jewelry in her hands. Her eyes were filled with tears and rage as she opened the door and threw all of it deep into the driveway and the front lawn.

"Yo, you willin' out? What is you doing?" I said as I grabbed hold of her and she attempted resist, until I reached past her and closed the door and she fell into my arms. I held her as tightly as I could, afraid to let go as I felt her body tremble, because I knew that it just might be the last time I got to hold her so close. Finally, she gave in to my embrace. With her head in my chest I heard her say, "We could have been so good together. I love you, Anthony, but I gotta...I have to let go! I can't do this and if you love me at all, you won't make this any harder because..., it's killing me!"

Letting go is truly a difficult task, but I was wrong and I really did love her, so with all the strength I could find, I held her a little longer and I let go!

A feeling consumed me that I would never be able to find the words to describe...I couldn't breathe!

Chapter Eight
The Message

nothing seemed to be the same anymore! I made a lot of attempts to let Victoria know that I would be there and that I loved her. We spoke only twice in the past month since all the shit happened and I felt like I was back in prison! Gangsta is gangsta and just the same, man, love is most definitely love!

I got lost in my own world and my plan to get the fuck out became that much more of a priority to me. I wasn't hurting at all financially and greed had been a downfall for a lot of good niggaz, or simply not having the courage to walk when you knew it was time.

The past two weeks alone have been reason enough to know that I was fighting against *time*, and I couldn't win because time possessed the power, the strength, of forever and I was definitely a momentary figure in a game that was much, much, bigger than me...

Thirteen days earlier...two of my spots were raided and the loss was minimal. Four days later, another one, but only this was some rebellious ass niggas this time and it seemed to be real personal! Two of my runners were rocked to sleep in a real vicious manner, and although they took over a hundred stacks and about eighty thousand in work, these niggaz were courteous enough to leave me with something...a message, in the form of a witness....

"So what exactly did this nigga say to you?" I asked.

"Them muthafuckas was poppin' crazy at the mouth, saying that *'we was warned'* and to tell *'Main Man'* that if he's as smart as I know he is, then he'll breeze and take heed to the fact that this is just a warning...only the beginning." Lil Mikey was shook up as he told me about how some muthafuckas came storming like black rain, forcing him to pay close attention to the details of the murder of his best friend, TyLew, and Shorty 140, (one-forty).

"Mikey, you ain't peep nothing on these niggaz at all?"

"Nah! Them cats was garbed up and every time I raised my head," he said as he pointed toward his eye and head, "they got type physical wit' them burners, but the strangest part about the whole situation is like how it seemed as if they knew, well at least the ring leader, he seemed to know his way around as if it was second nature and he had been there a million times. The two other cats was strictly 'bout they business, but everything that happened and everything this nigga said just seemed real personal like it wasn't even about the paper, but the caper, ya feel me?" he asked.

"Who did you call when you left?" I asked him.

"I called you. I was gonna call Ty's mother, but I figured that might not be the best move, but I don't want no crackas breaking the news to her. You know he was like my brother so..."

"I feel you, homie! Dig right, go to pay your respects and send my condolences. Don't call or talk to anybody else! You weren't there and that's how I want it to stay. *Here*." I pulled out a brown bag from the glove compartment and offered it to him. "Listen, there's close to thirty stacks in there. You take care of T.L.'s mother with any arrangements that need to be made. I know this shit ain't the easiest to deal with, but I'm glad that you here dog! You still wit' me? 'Cause if you ain't feeling this shit, I'll understand, but I need to know now."

"Ant, I'm good! I mean, I ain't happy about what happened, but I barely got my feet wet in this thing so I'm far from drowning. I hustle wit' a cause, not just *because*, so like I said, I'm straight."

"Square Business?" I said with my fist out.

"Square Business!" he responded, as he hit my fist with his.

"Well, let me smash out 'cause I have a feeling it's gonna be a long muthafuckin' week. You trying to get dropped off anywhere?"

"My whip is around the corner. Be easy, alright?"

"Yeah, you do the same lil nigga. I'm a holla at you before the week is over so we can find some shoes more suitable for you, 'cause what you did was real big, my nigga, and I respect that, so maintain until then."

"Alright! Cool!"

Here it was, a little more than a week since then and I was far from a detective, so I was lost. I set up a little extra security for my peoples and even though everybody said they wasn't worrying about that shit, I knew better 'cause you could reach out and feel the tension all around. I had put word out there that it was this lil team of niggaz from New York that did it, because they were already on the menu, so I figured it would be best to kill two birds with one stone and let all this fear of some type of war die with these niggaz! War and money on a street level don't mix, so you eliminate any problems before you allow them to become too big to handle, but it's impossible to do that when you have absolutely no clue as to where this beef is coming from or how it's coming so until I could figure that out, I wanted my people to breathe easy. I wanted whoever was responsible to think I really believed it was the cats from New York, so I used potential beef, as a source, for whatever people thought, and more importantly, as an example. Like I said, "Any type of sign of weakness would guarantee the vultures to start circling." If I didn't set an example quick and fast, it would have been perceived as exactly that...WEAKNESS! I just bought some time!

Chapter Nine
Baby Momma . . . Drama

"Trini Mon, what's happening?"

"You tell me, friend, it's been a while," he said.

"I need to speak to you up close and personal, and soon," I said.

"So I've heard. Listen, I've been planning a trip anyway so without details, we'll see each other soon!"

The line went dead. From the sound of things, this nigga already knew, but it really wasn't surprising. I had made my mind up to double up and try to make as many moves as I could as fast as I could and hopefully find out if Trini had his eyes open concerning my most recent unfortunate situations, because I damn sure didn't and I was willing to use anybody's resources to find out who! I would eventually find out why!

As I headed over to J.O.'s spot to hear whatever bullshit he had to tell me, my phone was going off.

"Yo, what's good?"

"You, playa, you might wanna shoot over to the hospital and see what's really good!" Big-Dee said with excitement.

"The hospital?" I wasn't hip to what he was saying.

"Yeah, nigga! My shorty just came home telling me that Kia been at the hospital for the past half hour, about to drop that load."

"Why the fuck that bitch ain't call me? How the fuck she gon' call ya shorty and not me?" I was tight!

"You know she been on some other type time since you cut her loose dog. After the word you gave me about what happened, shit, no disrespect, my nigga, but I wouldn't have called your ass either, but fuck all that, you about to be a daddy. Go handle yours, playa'!"

"No doubt. Good looking though for calling."

"Ant, congratulations, nigga," he said, trying to make me lighten up because he could tell I was vexed.

I rushed over to the hospital and as I drove, my mind wandered and took me back a few weeks thinking about how this broad was a snake in the grass...

"So, what happened?" Kia asked me, as I entered the door of the house about ten hours since I was on my way.

"What happened with what?!" I snapped, with Tori on my mind.

"Hmmmph...I guess that answers that, doesn't it!" She continued. "You know what? This shit is real corny. You got me over here waiting on you like a dizzy bitch and...this bitch calls you and you don't have the decency to call and let me know you ain't coming? Then you come in here and have the nerve to snap on me! Pssst, this shit ain't right."

She was right, but I was mad and hurt, so right then and there, she was irrelevant. Her feelings were too!

"Dig this here, I'll snap on whoever I wanna snap on and all that letting air out your tires, if you looking to get aired out, you definitely on the right path."

She knew I wasn't about putting my hands on no female,

let alone one who was carrying my baby, so she decided to take complete advantage of it too.

"Oh, so now you wanna fuck me up 'cause you're wrong! Nigga, you got the game fucked up 'cause you ain't gonna do a muthafuckin' thing to me, alright! You got me confused with your other *bitch*!"

All that emphasis on the word *bitch* was getting me tight! Every time she said it, I was reminded of the fact that I really didn't deserve Victoria, and it was my selfishness that forced me to believe that I was worthy of her. I knew that now wasn't the time to pursue a relationship, but I couldn't let go because I feared that I would lose her for good, so I let shit get out of hand. One thing for certain, she was innocent in all of this and this bitch ain't have no room to get out on her!

"No! You got *me* fucked up! I ain't gon' put my hands on you, you right! But all that fly shit you trying to pop, save it 'cause you ain't in no type of position to be screaming somebody else a bitch. The only reason *you* ain't on your fuckin' way is 'cause you carrying something that belongs to me. I let you trap me up but you can bet your life on..."

"Hold up!" she said interrupting me. "Trap you? Trap you! Imagine that! You wanted this pussy and I'm sorry to be the one to tell you, but there's more that comes with it. You'll have to excuse me for having a mind and a heart. See, you think the world revolves around *you* and it ain't like that. Do you think that all this is a coincidence?"

I stared at her, my eyes daring her to say what I feared she might say and, unfortunately, I was right, as she stood up and continued to speak through her tears. "Are you really that blind? No, I made it happen. I made sure your *wifey* knew about it! I mean, why shouldn't I have, since you seemed to find it necessary to remind me about her every other opportunity you got? Fuck that. I ain't playing second to no muthafuckin' body because it's convenient for *you*. Fuck that! You got a choice to make and I advise you to put some real thought into it 'cause I won't let you continue to play me *or* my baby!"

I was speechless. I couldn't believe that she was saying this shit, but at the same time, it shouldn't have been surprising at all! Finally, I said, "You fuckin' snake! You ain't worthy of the beats of your heart that allow your body to function properly, you dizzy bitch! What! You thought I would do some idiotic shit, like choose you? I know you ain't for real...Ha, ha...Oh shit! Look at you. You're serious, ain't you? When I met you, I put all the cards on the table and you chose to play your hand and now all of a sudden, you got a heart and a mind and you trying to reshuffle the deck! You just did some real grimy, shiesty ass shit and I told you, you ain't got but one time to cross me. You should've used it more wisely 'cause if I don't do nothing else on this earth, bitch, I'm gon' punish you! I promise you that!"

With that, I walked out and never looked back. Luckily, she ain't have no clue about my being wanted and any knowledge she had about my business was *real, real,* limited, 'cause females who feel hurt tend to go to any extreme to make you feel the same.

I knocked on the door to Kia's room at the hospital. The door swung open and I was greeted by a bunch of people who I assumed were her whole entire family. Of all of them, I had met only her mother and her cousin, Cherise, who had a real bad thing for me, and if she was about two or three years older, that would've been a mutual thing 'cause she was the spitting image of *Christina Milian* in the face, of *J-Lo* in the waist, but was only sixteen, but my bid was in for *future* references! The room got quiet all of a sudden and as people moved away from the bed to make room for me, I saw her. The most beautiful, precious thing I've ever laid my eyes on! Kia spoke to me, because I was in a daze.

"Do you wanna hold her?" she asked.

"Nah, I'm cool. I'ma just sit right here and watch."

I wanted to hold her, but she looked so small and fragile and at 6'3, 230 pounds, I was afraid to hold her for fear that I wouldn't be gentle enough and something would go wrong.

"Anthony, that's your daughter! Hold her! Come sit by me and hold *'our* baby.'"

"You sure?" I asked, as I eased up closer and reached out to receive my baby girl in my arms for the very first time.

"Of course, I'm sure. Here, hold her head like this," Kia said as she motioned with her own hands and arms like she still had the baby in her arms.

Everything that I had in me that was good created a 7 pound, 3 oz, 21 inch beautiful baby girl named *Tasaday Kiandra Fennell*. I held my second chance at life in the palm of my hands...literally!

After signing the birth certificate and taking pictures, which I, under any other circumstances would have been against, I went and shared my news with my team! For once, I did something that was worthy of all praise and congratulations and I wanted to hear all of the above! I deserved it! It's crazy, but holding my daughter, I forgot about the hate I felt for her mother and if only for that moment, I felt a connection with Kia that was as refreshing as a breath of fresh air. I began second guessing my judgement. How could I feel hate towards a woman who contributed to creating such a beautiful thing? In that hospital bed, she was beautiful. Too bad it was only a passing thing!

I was on my way over to meet up with Big-Dee when all the excitement and joy I was feeling was overpowered by a burden of guilt and sadness. Not once through the last few hours did I stop to think about Victoria. My pleasure was the cause of her pain! I've called a few times and we spoke, and every time the subject of *us* came up, she got aggravated so I did my best to refrain from the topic, but it's real hard to chase, especially when you're so used to being pursued, but love is a powerful, unexplainable thing!

I was gonna call, but decided against it! I felt the urge to see her, and regardless of what we agreed upon, I planned to do exactly that!

On the way, I stopped to cop some roses for her with a card that, for some reason, described everything I was feeling! It's funny how a card can describe what you feel but are unable to put into words. It said... *"Love!...Too little of a word to completely explain what I feel! An understatement...You represent every breath that I breathe...You are my life, my world...and without you, there could never be me!"*

Pulling up to her house, our house, I noticed a car in the driveway that wasn't familiar. A lot of wild thoughts flashed through my mind and I left the flowers in the car and walked slowly toward the door. I wasn't prepared for no bullshit, even if I did deserve it! *What a tangled web we weave.*

I backtracked and placed my burner inside the car 'cause it was better that way for me, *and* whoever was the owner of that two-year-old beige Expedition with factory rims on it, *Broke Muthafucka.*

I attempted to use my key, but the door was open. I slowly entered, hoping for the best! The house was empty as the day I purchased it. I immediately regretted leaving my burner in the car. I was caught up in the middle of a fucking burglary.

I was in motion, heading for the door when a voice caught me off guard and had me type startled.

"Do you live here?" the voice said.

I spun around and noticed a man in the entrance way between the dining room and the main living room with an envelope in his hand instead of a gun! That set my mind at ease, so I replied, "Yeah! I live here. Who are you and what the fuck you doing in my crib?"

"Whoa! I'm not here for no trouble!" he said.

I reached in my coat, faking the funk, but he didn't know I ain't have no burner on me, but his eyes told me he believed. So I said, "Then what the fuck you doing up in here? Where's my shit and where the fuck is Victoria?"

"Listen, no disrespect or anything, but I was paid to come here and leave these keys and this," he said as he waved the envelope. He continued, "I don't know nothing about no stuff being missing or no Victoria."

"Who paid you?" I asked.

"Some girl and her sister gave me a hundred dollars to come here to this address and leave the keys and this envelope on the bed upstairs. I was gonna leave it, I swear to God I was, but I just got thirsty and went to the kitchen and you came in. That's the truth." He was talking without breathing. I believed him!

What the fuck was going on? I couldn't understand why she would be doing something like this, but with her sister at her side, there was no telling what type of nut ass shit she could be talked into 'cause I knew for a fact, this wasn't Tori's work!

"You said her sister? And where did you meet them?" There was no longer any hostility in my voice. Just curiosity.

"She kept referring to her as sis, and I just assumed she was and I didn't actually meet them. They met me through my cousin and I needed the money so I just came to do what I was asked. Nothing more or less!"

"Is that right? Well dig this here, playboy, we got a new job assignment for you. This is how it goes. You performed your duty, so you're gonna call her and tell her that the key..."

He cut me off saying, "I can't call because I don't have no number. Like I said, I was paid to do something and that's all I come to do."

I started thinking before I spoke. *Why the hell would she pay a muthafucka to do what she could have easily done herself* and then it came to me. No matter our differences, she loved me and maybe she forgot to leave them and if she came back, she would realize the finality of what she was doing and she needed to be pushed when it came to matters of the heart! Otherwise, she would change her mind. I finally spoke.

"You say they paid you a hundred ones? I'll give you ten times that amount to holla at your cousin or whoever to find out where she's at right now...what's up?"

I saw his eyes jumping at the thought of a G. All that uncomfortability and fear turned into greed. It was too easy because I would have offered so much more.

"You mean to tell me that you're gonna give me a thousand dollars just to know where she's at? Are you trying to hurt her or something?" he spoke.

"Playa', I would never hurt something I love. If you know where she's at, it ain't gotta come back to you. There's a way around everything and if you second guessing the bread...," I pulled out about six thousand to show and prove and he bit...immediately.

"How do I know you're gonna really give me a thousand dollars?" he said, already knowing exactly where she was.

"Dig this here. I don't play no games about no money and my word is my bond so, the choice is yours."

He sat there fake thinking, like he was really contemplating something and said, "I ain't no snitch or nothing, but I'm trying to do what's best for me. She staying out the Radisson, room '532,' but you ain't hear it from me. You ain't gonna tell her where you got that from are you?" He was trying to act like he had some type of conscience or something. What a fucking joke.

"I gave you my word and that's more than enough playa'! Here, take this." I peeled ten hundreds and handed them to him and I explained to him that if it turned out to be bogus info, that there was no price I wouldn't pay or length I wouldn't go to in order to make sure I got my money's worth from him and he expressed his understanding.

"Now! Get up out of my house and let's do our best to stay out of each other's way," I told him.

I still had the envelope in my hand and I took a look around the house before I ended up in the bedroom. I sat there and took a deep breath as I opened it.

Dear Anthony,

How does one person truly express what they feel for another? Is it even possible? I've come to the conclusion that it's impossible, because I gave you everything and in turn, you've given me everything but that which I wanted or needed...you! I've come to the conclusion that what we are experiencing is commonly known as a "clash of realities."

Your reality being that you've been deprived of so much in life that you really don't know how to follow your heart because you're afraid of being let down or hurt in the process or the long run! You have experienced things that are uncommon and I understand why you feel the need to take charge of things and attempt to protect yourself. The worse part is that I know and believe that you are a good man, but you don't!

I met you and fell in love with you as if it were second nature, and under the most extreme circumstances, and I miss that man! Did he truly exist? Tell me, I was seeing things or playing make believe, because that's the man I wanted you to be. Tell me it was my fault and I'm wrong.

My reality is that I'm in love with a man who won't allow me to love him, completely and genuinely. I haven't lived your life, but I've allowed you to become mines and I don't think love is supposed to feel this way! You're having a child isn't even a factor because I know you didn't intend to do this. I can't afford to shed another tear while trying! Honestly, I'm afraid to keep trying because I fear that I might find out that this was all a game and I'm the only one who lost!

My heart is breaking and this pain is unexplainable...You promised never to hurt me. I can't do this anymore because you're killing me! I will always love you, God knows I will, but this is what's best for the both of us. Please, let this be! I'm not mad at you, Anthony, because I understand, but it hurts just the same. I'm not blaming you for anything because I accept the fact that I took a gamble and hoped for the best. Every little girl dreams of that one man who will move her, physically, mentally, emotionally and spiritually! You were my dream manifested in the flesh! I will never deny that, but I need to move forward because I'm no longer that little girl and that reality is harsh! I don't wanna hurt no more! I love you more than my next breath! Please let me breathe!

I adore you,
Victoria
XOXOXOXO

Chapter Ten
The Search for Lost Love

How do you let go of something you love? Here it was, the day of the birth of my daughter and I couldn't bring myself to feel anything other than pain. I was hurt! No bullshit, I was hurt and I sat there and read and re-read every word, every line, over and over trying to figure out what to do. She was right about everything and the *truth* really does hurt! I wanted to respect her wishes, but the selfish part of me—the part that told me I deserved her, wouldn't allow that, and once again, I only worried about my feelings and if the ends justify the means...fuck it, I'd be a selfish muthafucka!!

With that thought in mind, I made my way over to the Radisson to claim mines!

"May I help you, sir?" the desk clerk asked.

These hotels stay with a gay flamboyant type working the front desk. Fuck it, though, I wasn't there to judge anybody, so I responded very politely...

"Yes, my wife most recently checked in and my flight

was due earlier, but, unfortunately, it was delayed momentarily and I was told there would be an extra key awaiting me."

I caught him off guard with that one, but with a pair of six thousand dollar baby crocodile, reversible loafers on with linen slacks and a linen, short sleeve pullover to match, what else would he expect? I could talk my way into and out of anything. He spoke after thoroughly sizing me up.

"And your wife's name, sir?"

"Victoria Riley, room 532 if I'm not mistaken!"

I stood there and hoped he would do right and he did. The roses in my hand helped too!

"Well, that's not a problem. Here you go, sir. Enjoy your stay, sweetie."

This muthafucka was trying to flirt with me! Ain't that about a bitch! Being in prison, it was common to see a punk, so I smiled and kept it moving. I had things on my mind and I wasn't about to check this *Boygirl* and waste any more time. I rushed to the elevator and pressed five. I went to room number 532 and tapped lightly on the door, feeling like a fucking stalker or something! I stuck the key in the door and at that moment, her voice came through the door to ask who it was. I replied, "Room service, ma'am."

"Hold on a second," she said.

When the door opened, she stood there with a shocked look on her face and I walked by her because whatever words would be passed weren't for public display.

"Excuse me! Where do you think you're going?" was all she could come up with.

"Look, evidently you went to this extreme for a reason, so I ain't about to take up a whole lot of your time, but I do got some things to say and all that I ask is that you listen and I'll be on my way."

I had no idea what I was gonna say, but it had to be

good.

"I don't wanna go through this Anthony, I really don't, but you clearly ain't trying to respect my wishes so say what you gotta say but nothing is gonna change my mind. I'm telling you now!" She was trying her hardest to keep it icy and it definitely wasn't her style. I wanted to smile 'cause I saw through it, but I had to let her stand on her own two feet. I'd play around it!

Right at that exact moment, my phone went off and I had left the vibrate mode off, so she heard it and I went to answer it. She got up out of her seat and said, "You better decide what's more important, because we're on *my* time."

I had a quick flash thought of me doing some sucka movie shit like smashing my phone, but that thought came and went with speed! I simply turned it off and sat it on the nightstand and began to speak.

"I'm not sure if you know or not, but a few hours ago, Kia gave birth and I know that doesn't move you, but I just wanted you to hear it from me so you could understand that instead of being happy and celebrating, I felt really guilty because my happiness isn't the same if it ain't yours too! I made up my mind to come see you today and, you know the outcome of that, but there's no limit to what I would have gone through in order to find you. I know you got your reason for everything, but I read your letter and, baby girl, I don't know how to let go! I'm not gonna stand here after reading that letter and after knowing the woman you are and say it's easy for you 'cause I know it's not!"

She attempted to say something but I was already zoned out so I continued.

"I don't regret having my daughter, but I wish it would have been under different circumstances. I ain't a perfect man and I've never, not even once, professed to be one. I make bad decisions like any other man, but I didn't make a mistake or a bad decision when I fell in love with you! I can't change the past, but after everything we've experienced together, we owe it to ourselves to fight for our future! The same future we spent so much time talking about, wanting, and wishing for. I'm ready! I admit that I wasn't completely ready for all of this before, but I never told you 'cause I was afraid that you would leave, so I did what I had to, to hold you, knowing that I wanted all of those things, hoping it would happen sooner than later! Well, it's happened and all I need is for you to let me show you! I know damn well all of this wasn't in vain! I can't make excuses for the past 'cause don't a muthafuckin' thing make it right. You make mistakes and you learn from them. I refuse to make the mistake of letting you go! I refuse! Look at me. I'm afraid to stop talking 'cause I'm afraid that I ain't say enough or the right things, but one thing is for certain, this is my heart speaking to you!" I said as I pointed and poked my heart for emphasis!

She had her head down and I didn't know what else to do so I reached down and lifted her chin gently and saw her eyes full of tears. That hurt me! I got on my knees and laid my head in her lap like a child and it happened... She grabbed my head and began to caress my head and back, reaching for more of me, pulling my body up closer to hers..., closer!

"I love you, Tori, I swear to God I do! Tell me it doesn't have to end."

"I'm afraid," she said. "You don't know, this isn't right."

"Don't be," was my reply sounding like *'Floetry'*.

I kissed her softly on the forehead and tried to feel out her response. She tilted her head and said, "Anthony, promise me you'll be gentle, and I'm not talking about my body. I'm talking about my mind and heart. Promise me you'll do right by me!"

I kissed her passionately and between kisses, I said, "I promise," almost six times.

I was on top of her bed, realizing just how much I missed my boo. I meant every word I spoke! This was it!

We kissed like teenagers, wildly, wondering if sex was the next move. We had been away from each other for a minute and it all seemed like a new experience. Actually it was. Our love had reached a new level and sex with love is the most indescribable feeling! It makes a nigga wanna switch his vocabulary and say words like: *Wonderful, Gracious, Magnificent*...No Bullshit! I was gone!

I undressed her and kissed her tears and asked her to forgive me. She complied!

I kissed, sucked and nibbled on every inch of her beautiful body and watched as she went to another level with her body twisting and her back arching. I French kissed her pussy violently and her body jerked as I inserted my tongue into her and my nose rubbed up against her clit!

"I'm...oh, my God...I'M CUMMING."

She grabbed my head and tried her hardest to regain control by tightening her legs, but my hands gripped her inner thighs and spread them as wide as I could. I felt her muscles in her legs twitching and her body went limp. I looked up and everything from that point seemed to go in slow motion. Everything was magnified times ten on a sensual level! I climbed on top of her and let my dick rub up against her mound, rubbing up and down, my body getting tighter, trying to hold on to my composure, kissing her titties softly and gently. Slowly, I allowed myself the pleasure of her most inner secret treasure and her eyes rolled inside her head. She was to me at that moment, the most beautiful thing in the world! I drove deeper and deeper, climbing her body like a mountain straining to reach the peak!

"Oh, oh, mmm, oh," was all she continued to say. After

about twenty minutes, she screamed in a hushed tone..."Take what's yours. Oh, Daddy, please cum inside me...ohhh!"

I was sweating crazy like and I could feel our skin popping and my body jerked wild like as I came. I laid there, exhausted inside of her love. My body collapsed on hers as she stroked my head and back with the tips of her nails lightly like a feather. It sent chills through me and cooled me off as I began to feel breezes. For the very first time in my life, I made love to a woman that I knew loved me in return... Amazing is the word that semi-described the feeling!

Chapter Eleven
The Beginning and the End

We spent the next two days in room number 532 and talked, laughed and made love over and over again. I forgot all about the world. I didn't wanna leave because I was afraid to end what we started, but after checking my messages while Tori was in the shower, I knew I had to leave, hopefully not for long and hopefully she would truly understand.

Maybe she sensed it, but when she came walking towards the bed, she said, "Baby, it's gonna happen this time. It's now or never, but you can't prolong the inevitable. You gotta go see your daughter."

I was shocked, but this was the Victoria I fell in love with.

"Baby, I'm not mad. Just make sure you give her a kiss for me and you come home to Mommy."

I gave her my word and with that, I was on my way. I wanted to see my daughter, but a message from J.O saying he was in the county with a one hundred thousand dollar bail for fitting the description of a robbery suspect basically caught my attention, so after I called his bitch to see what the hold up was with his bail, I made my way over to Kia's house to see my baby! My daughter.

After about two hours, I made a few calls and made an arrangement with the bondsman to set bail. I was really a good muthafucka, 'cause it was more than he ever did for me when I was in the belly of that beast. I made my mind up that tonight, I was gonna pick this nigga up and one of two things was gonna happen, and neither of them consisted of him returning from that trip! I was cutting all loose ends in my life. No more procrastinating!

I parked two blocks away from the jail, inside my now champagne colored 600 Benz. J.O. already knew to meet me. I saw him walking towards the lot and I flashed my lights on him. He got inside the car and I asked him if he was straight to drive. He said *yeah* and we switched.

He thanked me and I basically shrugged it off as nothing and I knew that bothered him because a niggaz' conscience was bound to fuck with him.

"Listen, we got a problem that needs to be fixed," I said.

"What up?" He ain't know where I was coming from.

"I know exactly who been running up in the spots and who bodied T.L. and tonight, we gonna get back on the front line and make sure that debt gets paid in full. Ya feel me?" I said.

"Who? What's good? You know I'm with you, nigga!" He was excited for some reason.

"A week ago, I got word from the young bitch from the saloon that Bird and the cat Raw been running around wit' new found money talking crazy about how they spending real blood money. My lil bitch fuck wit' the nigga Raw like that, and to make a long story short, they did it, and I don't plan to let them do it again."

"Let's have it," was his response.

We went and gripped a squadder and my plan was to

leave J.O. stinking with these duck ass niggaz trying to swim in a gangsta's pond.

We didn't put any masks on! We dressed casually in black sweats and I had copped two F.B.I. jackets and badges about six months earlier just for the sake of having them, but now they would come to good use. We didn't plan on leaving any witnesses! No exceptions!

As we circled the block, we noticed no cars in front or back, so we laid on them close to the crib, but far enough away not to be noticed.

An hour of waiting paid off. Just as we expected, *Dumb and Dumber*, I mean, Raw and Bird pulled up and got out of their truck with some white bitch who looked like a vicious fiend. I knew they were about to try and freak the bitch, but I had something better that would literally blow their fucking minds!

"Let's move," was the first thing I said after an hour of uncomfortable silence.

We moved toward the house quickly enough not to draw any attention to ourselves. I knocked on the door and a bitch's voice came from the other side. "Who is it?"

"Police! We're looking for a *Belinda James*. Is she home?"

I heard commotion on the other side of the door, and just when I thought it would come down to me kicking the door in, it opened and the white freak stood there barely dressed, looking nasty as fuck. I flashed my badge and asked the question again. I looked past her and noticed these niggaz sitting at the dining room table fake playing cards trying not to look up, when she said, "Are you really cops 'cause you too fine to be a cop?" She smiled a funky ass smile that consisted of nothing but nastiness! "I think you have the wrong address, Officer Fine."

"No, I believe we have the right one." I brodied my way past her too fast for her to even respond. With my gun in hand, I ran up on them muthafuckas and they weren't hip until they saw my face up close.

"Yo! What the fuck is going on?" asked Bird.

I grabbed the pillow off the couch on my way to the dining room and before he could say another word, *BOOM*, I shot him in his head! The bitch started to scream, but was cut off with a smack to the back of her head by J.O.'s gun.

"I never liked that muthafucka anyway," I said.

As I aimed the burner at Raw, his eyes grew wide with fear, but it didn't change the outcome. *BOOM, BOOM.* His last sounds on earth were gargling sounds as he tried to choke himself to stop the blood from seeping out of his neck!

"I just killed two birds with one stone, well, at least one Bird, fucking Ducks!"

I looked toward J.O. and he cocked his joint and looked at me. I nodded as his gun went off into the bitch who represented the walking dead already.

I watched his face and something wouldn't let me do what I intended to do. I grew up with the nigga! I had love for him. Even through everything, I had love for the nigga!

We rolled out as casually as we came and as we drove, I cried to myself, not because of what we did, but because I was really about to kill my man! I froze up 'cause I couldn't do it! Would I live to regret it? God only knew, but I would take the bitter with the sweet until that time came!

When we pulled up to his Southside apartment, I got out of the car and told him we needed to talk. He agreed and we went up and I had some things on my mind. Questions that only *he* had the answers to! I watched him put his gun up on a shelf. I did the same.

He said, "I'll get rid of them in the a.m."

"Yo, we known each other a long time and since I been home, I feel like there's some type of animosity between us and recently, it seems like we been feeling and acting crazy uncomfortable around each other. So I'm coming to you like a man, as a friend, to find out what's what before one of us makes a real bad choice about the other."

I began to say more, but he felt where I was coming from and said, "I know how you feel! I been wanting to holla at you for a while too. It seems like ever since X, may he rest in peace, was murdered, you been keeping your distance from a nigga."

"No bullshit. I'ma say this once and hopefully you can clear the air...word is that you had a whole lot to do with that situation and I need to know what you know. Be honest with me, please, man!"

"I heard the rumor, but honestly, yeah, we had some things going on on the side and shit ain't work out, and I wished death on him for the way he came at me like I was a fuckin' lame or something, but murder? Nah, I ain't cut from that type of cloth that would even permit me to do some greaseball shit like that! X was my brother! Whether you believe it or not, C.F.I. meant something to me, and still does! Always will!"

"I had to say something and you don't know how I been feeling about the whole situation," I said.

"Nah, I know what you been feeling!" he said.

"Why you been acting funny style towards a nigga since I touched? I can't understand that. What's good?" I had to ask 'cause I had to know. He sat down and hesitated like he was about to respond. He gave me a look that said he wanted to say something but didn't know how. Just when I was about to ask again, he said, "I knew this was coming and the answer is complicated, so I tried my hardest to avoid it, but you know what? You deserve to know why. Ever since we was kids, you been my man and everything came easy to you as far as surviving in this game. I knew niggaz wasn't feeling me when you brought me around all the time at first, but you went to bat for me. I'm not supposed to be here. You the only reason I'm here! You wanted me to be here. How do you repay somebody for your life? I mean, yo, you was my hero in more ways than one and when you fell, everything and everyone changed. The first two years, I couldn't find the heart to even try my hand and I wasn't intentionally shitting on you. Believe me, I wasn't, but I couldn't do nothing for you and that shit fucked me up. I got love for you like no other and I knew you felt some type of way about me, but I swear to God, I was gutted! I started seeing some paper and it was new to me to be making it happen on my own. X was there, but he wasn't you. He always told me how you wrote him and asked him for money and what not and I just wanted you to write me one time and ask me for some bread! I know that shit sounds real bitch like, but I felt like I needed you to come to me for once so I could come to your aid for once. You understand?

"Yeah, I hear you!" I said, not completely understanding...

"Ant, you ain't ever holla and I really thought you had some animosity towards me about what happened. Dog, I was sleep and you stepped up for me. I owe you my fucking life! Then you come home and I called myself doing you a favor trying to put you on and just like that...," *Snap!* He snapped his fingers and continued..."everything was the same as before! You took control and took this shit to a whole 'nother level. Everybody fell into place and there I was, once again, the low man on the totem pole! That shit fucked me up and I ain't gonna lie yo, you deserve to be on top, but I was there before you got here, and it wasn't easy to deal with it! That's the truth! How can I ever repay you if you always on top? It ain't possible!"

I finally spoke and I even understood...

"Dig, homie, first and foremost, you don't owe me nothing! Simple as that, but if you felt or feel the need to repay me, all you gotta do is stay true and be a friend! I did what I did without hesitation 'cause I knew in my heart you would have done the same. That's real! I was hurt that you ain't holla at me and then on top of that, your name was in a lot of niggaz' mouths Up-North! *J.O. getting crazy paper, doing this, buying that,* and I was sitting up there hurting. It wasn't even about no money! A letter, a kite, some flicks, anything would have been good, but I didn't and couldn't understand why you felt I wasn't worthy of those things. A closed mouth don't get fed, and I had to know and I'm glad we got the chance to rap 'cause I hear you and I'm so real that I do understand! You ain't gotta feel no way about me. What's mines is yours, my nigga!"

I stood and extended my hand in peace and he grabbed it and pulled me into him and hugged and said, "Regardless of what you say, I love you, nigga, and I owe you, but I know how to pay you and I'ma do just that!"

"This game ain't the common denominator in our friendship! Don't ever think that! You my muthafuckin' man simple and plain. All this paper and this bullshit don't mean nothing to me 'cause I'd give it all away in a second to be able to go back, and for what it's worth, I don't have no regrets, my nigga! Since we rappin' and gettin' everything in the air, we had this conversation before, but it's no longer just words. After the New Year, *I'm out*. This shit ain't for me no more. Hopefully, if everything goes the way I plan, I'll have a wife just the same!" I smiled because I know I meant it this time!

"Anyway, I owe these people some time, and I'ma get it out of the way before it's too late and as far as business, you got it! My connect is thorough and I'ma put you on, and all I ask is that you be straight wit' him and my homie Dee. He a good nigga and I mean a *real* good nigga! Other than that, I want you to get where you trying to be and be smart enough to get the fuck out. Don't be greedy! I'm gonna tie up some loose ends and I'm on my way!"

"Damn! You serious. Yo, I respect that and I'ma do what you asked. I hope I can find my way out 'cause I don't see it. It may sound crazy, but I'm happy with being a ghetto celeb, you feel me? This is my world. It's all I know."

"Look, I'ma get up outta here, but remember this here, it's all we know, 'cause we ain't made the effort to look elsewhere. Hold ya head and I'ma holla in the a.m."

"One!"

I felt good as I drove on the boulevard that night heading home! For the next month, I remained true to my word and made a point to wake up next to my woman every single morning. I was spending a lot of time with my daughter. Everything was good as far as my relationship with La'Kia. We had an understanding that she had my daughter and on the strength of that alone, she wouldn't want for nothing, but any physical relationship wasn't a reality any more! My little girl was gorgeous and grown in her own way...demanding, but there was nothing she couldn't have when it came to me. I wanted my presence to be felt and that was one of the main reasons I made my mind up to get whatever time I owed out of the way! Better sooner than later!

Me, Big-Dee and J.O. got together as much as we could, not just for business purposes, but to simply kick it like homies do!

My only problem was convincing Trini to play fair with J.O. and it took a lot, but after we got through the matter of trust, we came to terms eventually and I made the trip to introduce the two of them personally. To my surprise, they kicked it like they'd known one another forever. That's what's up!

December came around and it was a real cold winter

already. Other than a few niggaz working for me getting popped, there wasn't too much drama. Bails and lawyers were paid and that was that! I even got notice from Y.T.'s lawyer informing me that there was a strong possibility that his case would be heard in the Supreme Court and everything was looking in favor of the case being overturned. I knew it was my time to make my exit. Everything was going too good! Maybe I was just feeling paranoid, but I've never had a real strong relationship with good luck! It was time to go and New Year's was twenty-one days away. *Twenty-one days too long.* I was going in hoping for the best!

I didn't want to go in, but it was long overdue, and although prison to me could only be represented by *death*, I had to be a man and stop running!

I wasn't completely sure that it was the best decision concerning Tori, but it was a chance I had to take. I heard too many stories in my time, and read too many books where a nigga didn't follow his first intentions and bad always turned into worse! I contacted my attorney and explained to him that I wanted him to be present when I turned myself in. He agreed that would be best and reminded me of the importance of securing my money. I appreciated the concern, but that was a priority!

I was going in at 10 a.m. to meet with my attorney and we would go from there. As far as I know, I had no other warrants other than from the state which really wasn't about nothing! The more I thought about it, the more I wished I would have handled it a while ago.

I was on my way over to Big-Dee's crib on the Eastside when my phone went off.

"Yo, what's poppin'?"

"You know what's good, nigga...80/20 your way. What's good, Boss?" The voice on the other end replied.

I wasn't sure exactly who it was, so I said, "Who this?"

"Damn, celly, you don't recognize a playa's voice when you hear it no more?"

"Oh, shit! What the fuck? What's good, playboy? Who on the other line?"

It was my old cellmate, Father-Born, from New Jersey, one of the flyest niggaz I knew. A thoroughbred to the heart and a player in every sense of the word. He basically contributed to a great deal of my having Victoria.

He could manipulate words like crazy. If game could be bottled up and marketed, he would see *Bill Gates'* type paper and I would be the first to invest in that stock. I asked who was on the other line because he was calling direct.

He responded, "One thing for certain, a free man don't need no three-way, Deejay, you feel me?"

"Yo, you out?" I said surprised, not so much that he was free, but more so because time definitely flies. Three years and some change!

"Out is a strong word, baby, and you know my style. I'm always in it to win it, ain't a muthafuckin' thing changed. But if you're referring to me being free, in every sense of the word! I been getting some real good reports on you and it's only right that a true genuine playa stays in the company of the same."

"You got me fucked up, playa! I ain't no player, I just happened to be blessed with *Boss Game.*" When I said that, he laughed hard as hell. This was my walkie Up-North. We put wild miles in lappin' the track and building in the cell about what to do and how to do it once we touched. We talked about damn near everything and in the process, a bond was formed that exceeded simply being associates or homies! This nigga was the last of a dying breed and because of me being out here in the world ripping and running trying to make and break a dollar, my communication with him consisted of two or three sentences and a few money orders. Respectable, but it didn't seem like enough. This was my man and truthfully, his timing couldn't have been more off, but to see him on the flip side of the pen was a priority...a must!

"Where you at, nigga, 'cause I'ma come see you A.S.A.P. It's been a minute and I definitely wanna get in your ear," I said.

"I'm coming to see you, *Boss Game*, so tell me where a small timer like myself can bump heads wit' a Boss?"

"Alright, dig this here. Meet me by the Red Roof Inn on McArthur Road. How long is it gonna be?" I asked.

"About 4:30 the latest. It's 3 o'clock now, I'm in the town, but I'm in the process of planting seeds with this bitch I used to know once upon a time. She forgot who the fuck I was so I'm doing my best to remind her, you feel me?" he said.

I was saying "Yeah" when I heard a broad in the background saying, "You see what I'm talking 'bout. You always trying to disrespect me. I ain't no *BITCH*!"

"Hold tight one second, Ant." He was on the phone with me but started checking his broad. He said, "Dig this, you simple ass bitch! As long as you in my company, don't you ever part your lips to correct what I call you or what I say! You ain't got no idea what disrespect is. You disrespected yourself for them six years. You chose to part from the company of a playa like myself. You disrespect yourself every time you open your muthafuckin' legs and try to find some false sense of love with one of them suckas you been fuckin' wit' out here and you still broke and struggling! Dreams don't pay bills and neither do thrills! You sitting on a gold mine and I'ma show you how to capitalize before it's all said and done. As long as you in my presence, you gon' be better than any of these bitches out here, 'cause you gon' be my *bitch*! But a *Bitch* just the same! You dig me?"

I was on the other line waiting for this broad to say some slick shit and to my surprise, she said, "Yes."

"Okay, pimp! I see you ain't slacking! Four-thirty alright," I said.

"Four-thirty it is. Until then, be easy!" was his response before the click.

I continued toward Big-Dee's spot, and my intention was to pick up the forty stacks he had for me and motivate, but I wanted this nigga to meet my man Father-Born. I know one thing, regardless of whatever, I had a date in the morning! I wasn't missing it for no one or nothing! Truth...at least that's what I thought.

Chapter Twelve
Trying Is Lying . . . I Tried

We all agreed, well, me and Dee, to shoot to the bar, *The Lounge,* and we would decide there what to do. I had taken Father-Born shopping and I spent about seven of the forty stacks Dee gave me. Nothing major!

At the bar/club, we laughed about a lot of things. It was easy for all of us to relate to the conversation, since we had all done a lil stretch Up-North. Prison was full of stories and wild muthafuckas! After a few drinks I could tell that Father-Born was starting to feel himself. It was understandable, even though he was released a month ago, he said this was his first time out! I told the nigga everything that had happened and my plans after tonight.

He said, "Playboy, I got nothing but love for you and I always knew you was gonna do the damn thing, but I can't lie, I ain't expect all that. Like I said, I got good reports on you and you know how niggaz talk just for the sake of being heard, so I just took shit for what it was worth. Congratulations on your lil girl and everything! But I can't rightfully sit here and condone no prison time, especially on

off

160

the voluntary side of things. As far as the broad, Tori, Victoria, or whatever, you know its like this here, you a man and can't a muthafucka force your hand to do other than what you choose to do, but marriage is some serious shit and if you ain't took the time to dig deep and find out every intricate detail of her life, good and bad, and come to terms with her past, present, and her hopes, intentions and dreams for the future, then you riding off of emotions and logic and understanding is playing the back seat! You destined for destruction, playboy."

I cut him off! "Nah, yo, she a good woman! Me and her came a long way since she first wrote me in '98!"

"Yeah, I respect that and all that, but you my main man and if I told you any differently, I wouldn't be a true friend, so dig this here. Here's a good woman! A woman who peeped your handle off the internet and chose to holla for whatever reason. She's what you want her to be, nothing more, nothing less, but was she a good woman before she knew you? I mean, in all reality, a woman's past plays a major muthafuckin' role in who she is today and who she gon' be tomorrow.

"Then again, maybe I'm wrong and maybe I'm drunk and I'm talking too much and this yak got me grooving and if that's the case, that's my bad and I wish you the best! You know how I deal with these broads and she just seem too good to be true and if she got a sister or a clone, I want in!"

We all started laughing! Yeah, it was official, this nigga was twisted off that yak....

I can't tell no lie. I wasn't feeling that shit, but that was just him and he had helped me once before when I called myself being in love with this bitch I was hollering at from New York! Stank Ass Bitch!

I told him and Dee about this after hours spot called the *BOOM BOOM ROOM* where anything goes when it comes to hoes. I figured he could appreciate that shit more than me!

Just then, I glanced towards the front door, trying to be aware of who was coming and going and I'll be damned if I ain't see this bitch come through the front door with some nigga!

"Yo, Ant, ain't that Kia right there wit' that lame ass nigga?" Dee asked.

"Yeah, that's her simple ass traveling backwards," I replied.

I threw Father-Born the keys to my 600 and told him and Dee to bring the car around front 'cause I wasn't trying to get caught up in no punk ass traffic.

Dee said, "Yo, you straight, nigga?"

"Yeah, I'm cool, fam. I'ma holla real quick and I'll be right out. Make sure that nigga don't wreck my shit."

"Got you. Be easy, alright?"

"Oh, most definitely. That shit ain't about nothing!" I said.

Yeah, I was faking, 'cause I wasn't feeling that shit even if we weren't together. She was my baby's mother.

When I walked up, I wasn't trying to violate the nigga, so I let her peep me and she excused herself, I assumed, or just walked away from the nigga.

"What's up, baby?" she said.

She was drunk or high, one or the other!

"Ain't shit. What's good?"

"I just came out with my friend to get a drink."

"Is that right?" I was biting my tongue, but playing my part.

She was searching for some emotion. "Nothing happening!"

I said, "Dig, you grown and everything, and you do you, but make sure you keep these lame ass niggaz away from my baby girl, you feel me?"

She never got a chance to respond. If it wasn't the fourth of July, it damn near sounded like it. One gun shot after another, everybody screaming and running away from the windows. We lost contact through the commotion. About twenty shots later it dawned on me that Dee and Father-Born were outside! The bouncers locked the front door, so I headed to the side entrance where some nigga tried to grip me up and kept telling me not to go outside.

"Man, get your muthafuckin' hands off of me," I screamed.

As I got through the door, the outside was calm and the only noticeable thing was the smoke from the cold coming from a 600 Benz that looked like mines. It couldn't have been mines though because this one had crazy holes through the doors and windshield. I got closer and slowed my pace as I noticed Dee's foot hanging out of the passenger side door. Father-Born was slumped down by the floor. Both of them dead! I blanked out for a minute and just kept walking. Where I was going, I don't know, but my daze was disturbed by the sound of Kia's voice.

"Ant, get in the car, come on, Ant. The police is coming. Come on, get in the car!" she yelled at me.

I kept walking and she finally drove her car to the corner and got out.

"Ant, listen to me, please! The police are coming and you don't need to be caught out here wandering around. Get in the car and I'll take you where you wanna be." She reached down and grabbed my hand and she was crying now. She pulled me toward the car and I went along with her. As we pulled off, my eyes filled with tears of anger and guilt and my mind set on murder. Two good brothers gone and I know in my heart that each of these bullets had my name written on it. What the fuck made me so special that

God felt the need to save me and prolong the inevitable?

My phone was going off like crazy, but the last thing I wanted or needed was some conversation!

Kia broke the silence and said, "Is there anywhere specific you wanna be?"

My head was by the window tilted toward the sky. I was lost in my thoughts and I felt a hand on mines and I gripped it and held it tight.

"I wanna see my daughter," I said.

"Okay," was her response.

We came to the front door and as we walked in, her aunt was asleep on the couch with some church televangelist shit on the TV and Kia woke her up. She looked like she was shocked to see me there. She spoke and I spoke and she was out the door within a few minutes.

Kia came out of the room and told me my baby girl was asleep. I went in anyway because I was feeling so fucked up that I needed to be reminded that I had some good left in me. My baby was the representation of that! She was my peace of mind. My proof that my existence was about something! Kia stood in the doorway and said, "I'm gonna leave you two alone for a while. I'm gonna get in the shower. Ant, are you okay?"

"I'm alright, yo."

Ten minutes or so had passed with me still staring down at her. She started squirming and I didn't wanna disturb her dreams, so I eased out of the room. I felt alone and that wasn't an easy feeling. I went to the bathroom to tell Kia that I was leaving. As I opened the door, steam rushed me and I looked down and saw her panties lying on the floor and something took over me!

I saw her silhouette behind the glass and my dick got hard instantly! Without second thought, I reached toward the sliding glass door and pulled back.

Kia asked, "What are you doing, Anthony?"

I just stood there staring at her body. Her skin was shiny and sexy from the water and her titties were moving up and down with her breathing as she waited for an answer. I just stood there staring! Evidently she knew exactly what I was doing because she stuck her fingers into her mouth and placed her back up against the wall and looked right back at me as she began to caress her breast and slide her fingers down towards her pussy. Her eyes began to flutter as she spread her legs wider and began to rub her clit.

"MMMM...ooooh...ooooh" were the sounds she made as she slid her fingers into her pussy. With her eyes closed, she didn't even see me take my clothes off. I eased into the shower and began to suck on her shoulder, biting down as she moaned more. I rubbed my dick up against her and she reached down to grab it. As I held her titties in my hand and squeezed and sucked harder, she stroked my dick and said, "Oh, I missed you! I missed you so fucking much...mmmmmm, Daddy! Please, fuck me...mmmm... please, Daddy!" I grabbed a handful of her hair and pulled her head back and kissed her violently as our mouths slid off of each other's from the water. I placed my hand behind her left knee and threw her leg up as far as I could get it. She reached down and guided the tip of my dick into her pussy that was soaked by now. Once I felt the head enter her body, I thrust forward and shoved every inch of my dick into her. She screamed and I continued to fuck her with crazy passion. She scratched my back and dug her nails into it! The harder I fucked, the harder she scratched and screamed! I let her leg down and pulled out of her with my hand still gripping her hair. I directed her towards the floor. She looked up at me as the shower water beat against my back and began to suck my dick. She moaned while she ate my dick up with precision! "Cum for me, Daddy, cum inside my mouth," she said, and after another minute or two, that's exactly what I did!

I stood there with both hands on the shower wall breathing real heavy and Kia began to wash me from head to toe with a bar of soap in her hand and it felt too good! She continued to rub my balls and my dick. She dropped to her knees behind me and reached her right hand around and stroked my dick. With her left hand, she parted my legs wider and I felt her head between my legs as she started to lick my ass. I jumped and she said, "Relax, baby," and I took a quick mental note. *She wasn't doing this type of shit before. New lessons.*

I had never experienced the feeling before, but a nigga can't lie, that shit felt good as fuck, but I wasn't with it 'cause it made me feel weak. I had heard about that shit, but to actually experience it was crazy! I turned around and walked out of the shower and she followed, soaking wet, to the bed. She laid on her back with her 'fuck me eyes' and I grabbed her legs and flipped her onto her stomach. I gripped her by her hips and onto her knees and laid my hand on her back to push her face down into the mattress. I watched my dick glide into her pussy! I spread her ass cheeks, pulled out and rubbed the length of my dick over her asshole and shoved it right back into her pussy. I licked my finger and with that and the juices from her pussy combined, I began to insert my finger into her ass. Her body trembled and I felt her legs begin to buckle as I eased my finger in and out of her ass at the same exact pace that I fucked her. I spread her legs farther apart with mines and grabbed the base of my dick and eased up a little higher and placed the tip on her asshole.

"No! No, baby, not that. I can't."

"Shhh. You relax! I'm not gonna hurt you, alright."

"It's gonna hurt! ... Aaaahg, oooooh, it hurts, Daddy!"

"Relax, I'm gonna be easy. I want all of you. Will you

give me that?"

"Be gentle, please. Go slow...ooooh, damn! Shit, oh! Don't put no more in."

"I'm almost there. You're gonna feel good. Try to relax!

She bit into the pillow and tried to drop her body down flat on the bed so I stayed with her, talking smoothly and soothingly as I grinded my way all the way inside of her. With slow, one, two and three inch strokes, I worked my way in! She reached back to grab the back of my head and began to moan as she attempted to meet my every stroke. "Oh, God! It hurts!...It hurts so fucking good...do it a little harder...fuck my ass...oh, oh, oh, God, Daddy, Daddy, I'm cuming, I'm gonna cum...hmph. Ooooh, yes, yes, fuck me...oooh, aaah!" Her body went limp along with mines and I laid on top of her heaving and sweating, regretting what I just did! *Damn!*

"Anthony, I don't know what happened. I mean, I know what happened and I think I know why, and I don't want you to feel bad about it because I understand and I love you regardless of what you feel for me." She was reading my mind. How? I don't know!

I eased up off of her and didn't reply and went to the bathroom to wash and get dressed. When I came out of the bathroom, she was sitting Indian style with a pillow hugged between her arms. She looked up and I saw that she was crying.

"Listen, Kia, I don't feel bad! It happened and we can't take it back. We got caught up, but I love her and that can't change. Can you respect that?"

"Yes!" she replied.

I came over to the bed and kissed her on her forehead and with that, I made my way to the door. There was nothing more to be said and I had to get away and face my reality! One thing that became fact overnight..., I couldn't make that meeting in the morning. I just couldn't do it!

Chapter Thirteen
It's Hard To Say Goodbye

I called Victoria only once in the past three days! I was a master of making bad situations worse.

The last three days were spent with J.O. attempting to get everything in order for Dee and Father-Born. I was tired of the funeral scene and all the mourning, so after offering my sincerest apologies and deepest condolences to their families, I made my mind up that I didn't wanna deal with death any more, other than my own! No disrespect, but I loved them niggaz but I couldn't attend any more funerals and viewings.

The police caught the muthafuckas who did it at an apartment on 9th Street. The same night. The motive was still up in the air and I didn't know either one of them by name or face, so I had no idea about why! Animosity and hate seemed to never be represented by its original source and snakes as well as rats came in all shapes, forms, and fashions! They all flocked together though, which is only right because in the animal kingdom, rats hang, live and play only with each other and snakes do the same with snakes. No other creature plays with them! Scum of the fucking earth! So, it's only logical that lames fuck with lames and suckas fuck with suckas!

J.O. was all that I had left and he stood by my side everywhere I went, worried that anything could happen. He said, "If it happens to you, it's happening to me, no rap!"

I respected that! I was feeling type fucked up behind the fact that if niggaz wasn't fucking with me, none of this shit would have gone down like that! X, T.L., my homie, Big-Dee, and my man, Father-Born. I thought I was doing everything right. I was the way, the truth! I was everything but!

I wanted to see my daughter, but Kia had taken her to her mother's house in Atlanta. I knew she was only trying to go because she was feeling some type of way about the situation that transpired between us, but it was best that she left to so-call *spend the holidays with her family* because I didn't know what I was gonna do, and I didn't want her or my daughter in harm's way!

I played J.O.'s crib real close and he began to see the pain I was feeling! He said, "Dig, homie! I know you hurting and as fucked up as it is, you can't change what's done! You ain't did nothing but be good to niggaz and with this life, death is a high probability and you already know that. You had a plan and I admire you for even thinking about it, but maybe it's time to be good to yourself and do what's best for you! You can't save muthafuckas, but you can save yourself. I don't believe I'm even saying this shit, but maybe it's time for you to act on your plans!"

He was right! I was just procrastinating, afraid to say goodbye!

"You know what? You're right, and I'ma do that! Before I do, I'm going to get fucked up one last time until they have last call, you feeling me?" I asked.

"Am I feeling you? Nigga, I'm wit' you. Let's have it!"

was his response. "We gonna do it big tonight."

I found a new boost of energy! I went and got my Range out of the garage and prepared for my last night on the town. I went and got my hair braided and a shape up to match and I got dressed in a spanking charcoal two-button *GianFranco Ferre* suit with a pair of black gators with the belt to match. I put my three-and-a-half VVS1 on my pinky and a little bit of Vera Wang cologne for men. I was definitely treating myself tonight! No bars! No clubs! I was going to *Fantasy Isle*, a place where players meet and hustlers greet!

"Yo, who this?" my phone had gone off.

"How we gon' do this? Your ride or mines?" J.O. asked.

"I'll meet you there in a half. You ready?" I asked.

"You now how I do, fam! I'll see you there."

"One."

As I pulled up to the entrance, I saw some of the baddest bitches and the flyest niggaz and I felt good because I knew this was where I belonged. The valet gave me my ticket and I was feeling real good so I hit him with fifty ones! There must have been a lot of that going on 'cause he showed no emotion. I made my way to the entrance, paid my way and I spotted J.O. talking to a bunch of females who were listening to whatever he was saying so attentively that if I ain't know the nigga, I would have thought he was giving some stock tips away!

"Hey, this my man right here. Ant, I want you to meet Brandy, Lisa, Shaunte and Cherise."

"How you ladies doing tonight?" I asked.

"Fine," they all responded in sync.

"I got a booth reserved for me and my partner, Ant, and it would most definitely be a pleasure if you beautiful ladies would join us for a while. What do you say?"

The next thing I know, we were all in the booth and bottles of Dom P. were being popped. Myself, I ain't want nothing but a bottle of Remy VSOP, so I ordered two just in case!

Even the waitresses or hostesses were pretty. The broads at the booth were silly as fuck, and the more they talked, the more they exposed themselves, *and* the more I drank. The lights were dim and the music was on point. Mostly R&B and jazz! I wasn't real big on jazz, but it was real mellow! I liked it!

People came up and introduced themselves and everyone was just enjoying themselves. Unfortunately, after the first hour, that just wasn't the case with me. I was twisted and I excused myself from the company of a beautiful bitch named Cierra 'cause my mind was working overtime. I was ramming, feeling real fucked up like *Tony Montana* in *Scarface*. I began to wonder if this was what it was all about! Here I was, up like crazy *financially*, nice cars, beautiful homes, my choice of bitches, at least for a night, and I was feeling fucked up! Too much lost to make all that a reality and truthfully *all that* wasn't really shit!

"What's good, family? Everything alright?" J.O. asked as he walked up on me.

"Nah, yo, everything is fucked up, but it's cool. It's time to make my exit, man!"

"What you trying to do, head back to the spot? You sure you ready?" he asked, picking up on what I was saying.

"It's now or never, baby boy! Dig, you stay and enjoy them bitches, 'cause they definitely trying to enjoy you," I said with a wink and a smile. We shook hands and embraced and I told him to *stay up*.

"You do the same, nigga! I mean that. I'll see you when you need to see me."

I got one last look around and stepped outside. I handed the valet my ticket, and as I stood there waiting, the only thing I could think of was Victoria, hoping that she would understand and that we would be able to make it work between us! Nothing was promised so only time would tell!

I got into the Range and a song was playing by *Pac and Big*. I had only heard it here and there, but I never really paid attention to the lyrics before until now. The hook was my thoughts, my feelings...

"Why am I fighting to live, if I'm just living to die?

What am I trying to see, when there ain't nothing in sight?

Why am I trying to give, when no one gives me a try?"

I sat in the truck and listened to those words and I began to feel it! I dialed a number and Tori answered on the fifth ring.

"Hello, who is it?" she asked.

I paused for a minute and finally spoke. "It's me, baby! How you feeling?" I waited for a response, but I didn't get one.

She said, "Babe, why haven't you called me? I been worried about you. I read about Dee and I'm sorry! I know he was your friend."

"Yeah, he was definitely that! Listen, I know I been outta touch, but I haven't been myself lately and I needed some time to get my mind right. I been putting a lot of shit together in my mind and I'm seeing things real clear for the first time in a long time. I wanna see you!" I said.

"Boo, I understand! You don't have to ask to come home because it's always here," she said.

A smile came to my face! "I'm on my way and I should be there in about an hour, alright?" I said.

"I'll see you then," was her response. Then she added, "Anthony, know that no matter what happens, I do love you! I always will!"

That made me step down on that long pedal a little harder. Ain't shit like going home to the comfort of a good woman! Truth. I wanted to see her before I went to turn myself in. I needed to make sure home *was* and always will be home!

As I drove, I didn't even feel no stress. I was doing the right thing...for once!

I took in the scenery, hoping I would only be away for two years at the most. It was up in the air!

That was about the light end of it because ever since the *Mudman* situation, the state had been coming down real hard on violent offenders. Mudman was a convict who was part of one of the most known biker gangs, *Hell's Angels*. He wasn't supposed to come up for parole, but somehow he did, and although there were a lot of stories about how he did, stories are stories. He made it to see parole and the board slipped up and released him. To make a long story short, it didn't take him long to go home and kill a cop! I'm not mad at him because the parole board messed up. They felt the need to punish any and everybody who came up for parole with a violent crime. My release was unbelievable and it's not that it wasn't appreciated, I just couldn't deal with being semi-free! I'm an extremist, so everything with me is *all or nothing*! There're consequences and repercussions for everything. That's the laws of nature, and I was prepared to deal with them, however minor or extreme they may be. Fuck it!

Chapter Fourteen
A House Is Not A Home

Pulling into the driveway behind Tori's car, I placed the Range in park, and as I eased up a little more to take the keys out of the ignition, I glanced up and saw Victoria looking out like she always did. I smiled and she did the same! She was every bit of gorgeous! She closed the curtain and I went to reach for the door and it happened way too fast!

The brightest lights, so much commotion, that it took me a moment to realize exactly what happened.

"F.B.I., put your hands on the steering wheel...NOW!"

I was in a daze. My heart stopped for a second. Everything was in slow motion, even though it happened so fast. I closed my eyes to make it go away, but when I opened them, the same lights, the same commotion, the same men in black vests with yellow letters with guns drawn...it was real! *Was all this for me?* I'd never seen so many guns.

I placed my hands on the steering wheel and took one last glance toward the window, but she wasn't there. I needed her to be there! My eyes closed again...

"F.B.I. Step out of the vehicle with your hands up, slowly!"

I knew I didn't have it in me to surrender without a fight. They were here for a reason and whatever it was, it was serious, so the consequences would be the same.

I let my right hand slip down off the steering wheel onto my lap as I hyped myself up to take hold of the glock 40 that was on my hip! I gripped it and placed the barrel between my knees and held it in place as I cocked it back to place one in the chamber. I looked around and saw a sea of white faces and promised myself that I wouldn't even attempt to run, and that I would empty each bullet no matter what the outcome. I knew I didn't have a win, but I planned to leave my mark. A blaze of glory! What the fuck was a *Blaze of Glory*? Where was the glory in death?

My legs began to shake and I began breathing real hard and heavy and I began counting down with the glock in my open palm, each second representing another finger closing around the gun. *Five*...my pinky closed around the handle...*Four*...my ring finger followed...*Three*...my middle finger, my *fuck you* finger joined...*Two*...my thumb eased around the back creating a balance. *One*...my pointer finger found its way to the trigger...

I opened the door swiftly and in the same motion I stepped out and let the first shot off even before my foot hit the ground. I just kept shooting and yelling..."*You put your fuckin' hands up!*" They answered with a hail of gunfire that could never be taken back. Each bullet that struck me caused my body to jerk sending me down to one knee, where somehow I found the strength to raise it. I don't even think it was intentional. I was still fighting and I didn't want to, but it was happening! I couldn't let go. I was choking on blood and the heat was unbearable!

There I was lying face down on the cold grass, staring at a tire and a rim, with no strength left in me to shift my eyes. Life was passing through me with each breath I took, and I could no longer hear anything...no more gunfire, no more noise or commotion...it was gone! I could hear my heart beating loudly and rapidly like a drum in the Congo! My thoughts wandered...it was true, your life really did flash before your eyes. I saw my homies, my beautiful daughter looking up at me with her legs kicking and a smile on her face, and I saw my baby girl Victoria. All of the above being *my life*. Those things worthy of living for!

I felt relief, a true sense of peace. I felt light all the way through. No more stress. No more madness...no more pain!

"THIS IS YOUR LAST AND FINAL WARNING! Step out of the vehicle, slowly, with your hands in sight," the familiar voice screamed through the bullhorn.

My eyes opened! The same sea of white faces. I regretted not having the heart to make my dreams and flash fantasies a reality! There was no escaping the inevitable! I've told myself, as I'm sure a lot of niggaz have done in the past, that I *would rather hold court in the streets and let my banger represent me than to be brought back to prison on a new case* because new time meant new figures...*football numbers*.

Believe me, it was much easier said than to actually be done! I toyed with the thought for a second, but only a second. All those guns looked like the United States Army was outside and I wasn't ready to go up against an army with a handgun! I couldn't do it!

Somehow my hand slowly made its way to the handle and the door opened. I stepped to the concrete and followed every order to a tee! They rushed me, and once I was handcuffed and laid face down with a foot in my upper back, so many thoughts of possibilities came to mind about why it came down to this. I had done so much dirt and there really was no telling! Everything in darkness is eventually brought to the light! I was assed out!

I laid in the cold for twenty minutes before I was brought to my feet and a black agent approached me with a camera snapping pictures. I didn't even resist! What was the use? I fucked up!

An hour or so later, I was in the back of a black van, laid out on the floor getting my cuffs around to the front of my body. They had searched me for guns evidently because I still had a blunt in my breast pocket of my thirty-one hundred dollar suit. I figured I was facing charges that were so serious, that there was nothing to lose. I reached into my pocket and placed my blunt to my lips and searched my pockets for a lighter and finally, just when I was about to be upset and give up on my search and chalk it up to my having no fucking luck, I felt a lighter in my pocket. I got it and lit my *EL'*. I sat there and smoked that bitch like it was the last on earth! That good green was truly from God! Even in the worse type situation, I was grooving, feeling myself. It was over for me! The end of what, I didn't now, but most definitely the end!

When the doors opened and the light hit my face, I just smiled and watched the smoke go out into the air and disappear. I wished I was that smoke.

"I hope you enjoyed yourself 'cause it'll be your last! You can take that to the bank," a pale-faced officer said as he reached up to assist me out of the van.

"Don't you bet on that, Opie," was my response. "I want my lawyer contacted."

"Your days of making demands are over, so shut the fuck up!"

I could tell it was gonna be a long day! Ten hours and two cheese sandwiches and a milk and damn near a million thoughts later, I was escorted down a corridor toward a room with a phone. I called Victoria immediately! Twelve rings, twelve long ass rings later, I realized she wasn't home. She was probably on her job contacting my people and my attorney...I called J.O. again. No answer! I started to call La'Kia, but after the second ring, I decided against it.

There I was, alone in a room, feeling alone in the world! I assumed that my attorney had to have been contacted by now, but I called anyway...no answer...I left a message letting him know that the Feds had snatched me up and I needed him to show me that my paper was put to good use!

I looked back as the door opened and I saw a familiar face. I knew him, but from where, I didn't know. I hate that shit!

As he escorted me toward the holding cell, we passed other cells and all but one were empty. I glanced to the left and saw J.O. and he saw me, but neither of us spoke because if we were both here, it was best that we didn't acknowledge each other.

Once I heard the door at the end of the corridor lock, I placed my back to the bars because there was a camera out in front of each cell, and I called J.O. by his handle.

"Cypher."

"Yo, what the fuck happened?" was his response.

"Put your back to the bars, so they can't peep us talking," I said.

"Ant, what's going on, man? These muthafuckas came and snatched me up in my house!" he said sounding worried.

"Listen, I don't know what's going on! I called wifey and she ain't answer, so she probably trying to get my lawyer. I left the club to go see her and I ain't make it but to the driveway and these crackas ran all up on my shit like I was *Osama*. I know one thing, whatever it is, we here together so it's some shit in the game, so as far as these people are concerned, we keep it like this...we don't fuck wit' each other and we haven't since I came out. You know how they get down, so even though I know I ain't gotta say it, I'm a say it anyway. *No matter what they say or do, you stick to one story and I'll do the same. You feel me?"* I asked.

"Yeah, I feel you! Damn! This shit got me fucked up! Do they give you a call?" he asked.

"Yeah! I told you I tried to call wifey. It took long as fuck, but they let me try my hand. Dig, homie, you my man and you ain't ever been in this type of situation before so keep what I'm telling you in mind. These muthafuckas is gonna come at you with wild numbers and try to get you to cross niggaz up wit' wild time. This is where all that real shit and *souljaizm* comes into play. Pressure busts pipes or it makes diamonds. Now's the time to shine, Souljah!" I said trying to keep the nigga on point!

Before he could say anything in response, the key turned in the door and the footsteps got closer.

"Turn around and cuff up," the same muthafucka that I thought I knew said to me.

When we walked past J.O., I winked at him to let him know everything would be alright. He nodded his head lightly enough to not let the nigga peep!

I was taken to another room with a phone and a glass. Once the door was closed, the cuffs were removed and the nigga said, "Attorney Visit! He'll be up in a minute."

I sat in the chair and ten minutes had passed when I finally looked up and saw my attorney come in on the other side.

I checked his facial expression to try and figure out the seriousness of the situation. It was definitely serious!

"I wish our next meeting could have been under different circumstances!" were his first words.

"Who you telling! What's going on?" I asked, trying to

find out why I was being held captive.

"Well, it's not actually a simple explanation. What I do have so far is the fact that an indictment was brought down last week against you and evidently thirteen other individuals. The charges are very serious!"

"What are the charges?" I asked as I squirmed in my seat; reality was a few words away and I felt fucked up.

"Unlawful Conduct Relating to Influenced and Corrupt Organizations."

"What the fuck is that? You got to speak in plainer terms, man!"

I wasn't understanding, so he said with one word, "RICO."

"*RICO!* Man, they got me fucked up!" I said getting a little loud.

One thing for certain, *RICO* was the last thing any hustler wanted to hear! I didn't know the legal terms, but I knew that a four letter charge was the answer to a four letter sentence...*LIFE*!

He did a lot more talking and no matter what he said, my mind was stuck on them four letters! I never even really contemplated the possibility. *How the fuck did I turn a punk ass violation into forever? How the fuck could I have thought I was smart enough to do what I was doing?* All the foul ass shit that's happened over the last few years seemed like a movie, a lifetime script. *Why the good niggaz always get killed or end up in prison in the movies?* Their sentence only lasted two hours, depending on the length of the movie. *How does a nigga even begin to do life?* Yeah! They definitely got me fucked up!

My attorney finished by explaining the process about where I would be held and court appearances and I wasn't concerned with nothing but one thing, so I asked.

"How much is it gonna cost to get this shit up off of me?"

"I wish it were that simple. Believe me I do, but it's not! I can tell you as your attorney I'm obligated to inform you that the Feds are a different type of system. They'll come with a million years, and apply as much pressure as they can and more, and when it seems like they've applied enough, they'll come to me to offer you a lighter sentence in exchange for testimony."

"Whoa! Dig this here. I appreciate you letting me know what's up, but understand this: my life might not be the greatest, but there's nothing, and I mean *nothing*, that these muthafuckas could give me and have me go out of character so I could contribute to they fucking cause!" He knew I was serious! He claimed to have understood and even said he respected it. I wasn't supposed to discuss nothing with nobody because from the way he described it, *NOBODY* could be, *or* should be, trusted! I was sick!

I never saw J.O. after that. I spent the next two weeks in a Federal Detention Center stressing like crazy! It took about six days to receive my pin number to use the phone. I called Victoria every day and no answer! Now wasn't the time for people to start acting funny! I talked mostly to Kia, and for some reason, in all the time that I knew her, I never took her serious on a mental note, and she was showing me every day that she was really a good woman in her own way. She was extremely supportive and I didn't feel guilty about it! Maybe it was the situation at hand, or I was just delusional or something. Who knows! Whatever it was, I needed that support. I just wish it was coming from somewhere else, but glad it was here just the same!

I had been to court for arraignment where my charges were read to me and my bail was denied due to my being a flight risk. Not that it mattered, because I had a detainer with the state anyway so it wasn't surprising. I was stuck! I could have been the star in a *Snickers* commercial 'cause I definitely wasn't going anywhere for a while! *A while* seemed like an understatement!

According to my attorney, they had witnesses popping up from everywhere willing to provide testimony. He told me that J.O. was out on bond for a hundred and fifty thousand dollars, but he wasn't aware of any deals made or in the process of being made. I figured his criminal record wasn't major so he was eligible for a bail!

He gave me a copy of the indictment, and when I got back to the detention center, I went to my cell and read all twenty-three pages! I knew it was over! I was stuck on page two for a long time because I had never imagined a paper with those charges with my name on it!

Count 1. Conspiracy to participate in a racketeering enterprise. (Class A Felony)

Count 2. Conspiracy to violate the federal narcotics laws. (Class B Felony)

Count 1-1. From January of 2000 to December of 2004 (Anthony Fennell) together with others unlawfully conspired to violate the racketeering laws of the United States, in that he agreed to participate in the conduct of the Enterprise Affairs through the commission of racketeering acts, as set forth in racketeering act one through six.

Racketeering Act #1.(A) Conspiracy to distribute and possess with the intent to distribute cocaine

Racketeering Act #1.(B) Conspiracy to distribute and possess with the intent to distribute cocaine base

Racketeering Act #2.(A) Distribution of cocaine

Racketeering Act #2.(B) Distribution of cocaine base

Racketeering Act #3.(A) Conspiracy to murder Samuel Rockmore

Racketeering Act #3.(B) Murder of Samuel Rockmore

Racketeering Act #4.(A) Conspiracy to murder Michael Thomas

Racketeering Act #4.(B) Murder of Michael Thomas

Racketeering Act #5.(A) Conspiracy to murder Matthew Payne

Racketeering Act #5.(B) Murder of Matthew Payne

Racketeering Act #6.(A) Conspiracy to murder Susan Light

A long list of madness! How was it even possible for these people to know all this shit? It was as if they had a camera or some type of chip inserted in me from the day I was released from prison. Was the Fed shit really that serious? I had met a few cats up in the detention center and every once in a while I had heard some real wild espionage type stories concerning niggaz' cases and indictments and it was all new to me. I was told that nothing should surprise me dealing with these people, but each and every time I was! *Amazed*.

Three-and-a-half weeks had passed when I was called to the counselor's office. She told me that there was a death in my family and my uncle had called to have me call. He left a number. I wasn't worried 'cause I had no uncle, at least not one that would go out of his way to find me to inform me about a death, so I knew it was just somebody trying to reach out.

I explained to my counselor that I had burned up all but seven of my three hundred minutes and she granted me a call. I was hesitant at first because she was probably gonna be all in my mouth, but fuck it!

"Yo, just look serious and don't say nothing unless you talking about a funeral, alright!" It was J.O. I wanted to smile, but I played my part and said, "When did it happen?"

"Listen, my nigga, I ain't sure if you know, but they gave me a bond and right now it's a lot of bad blood out here. I sent you a stack today and I'll get something else to you

A.S.A.P., but yo," I just continued nodding my head asking dumb questions while he spoke and he went on...

"I ain't built for this shit, homie! My lawyer talking crazy figures, so I'm thinking about bouncing! Besides the fact, niggaz is feeling some type of way right now."

"About what?" I asked.

"We shouldn't have done that shit, Ant. We fucked up," he said.

"What happened?" I asked, curious as hell!

"Them niggaz, Mike and Sam, we shouldn't have killed them!" he said.

"I don't know them," were my last words to him before I hurried to hang up the phone! Immediately! I knew one thing to be true. That was the very last time I would ever speak to him!

I left out the counselor's office and she stopped me to ask if everything was okay.

My reply was simple as I walked out..."No!"

I had just learned my fate without a trial! I know I should have never second guessed myself. I should have killed that muthafucka a long time ago! It don't pay to be working with emotions when you up to your shoulders in this game! What really had me fucked up is how I knew all this shit. Never expect another muthafucka to do, simply because *you* do! *Real* is, everything just ain't for everybody! *Truth*.

This nigga actually tried to cross me up on a phone! He really had no respect for my ability to exercise my mind. I felt like kicking myself in the ass...literally!

Where the fuck was my woman? This *good woman* who was able to do what many others have tried and failed to do. She captivated my mind *and* my heart!

I called and continued to call repeatedly, feeling like some type of mental case. I hung up each time with worry. Wondering if she was okay!

The New Year had come and passed and this was the very last place I expected to be! You always get what your hand calls for. I was speeding out there getting caught up in my own world. The same thing I told myself time and time again. Not that it's not good to plan, but as solid as my plan seemed, my present situation was proof that there's always fine print that a nigga never takes the time to go over thoroughly!

I had seen my daughter twice since being there and I didn't like the fact that she had to see me like this, but I needed to see her. Each time was hard to deal with because it caused me to think more than I wanted to! *How does a man be a father from behind a wall? Would she love me and respect me the same as if I were free?* Having a child wasn't my intention, but unlike most aspects of my life, I had no regrets when it came to her!

I was in my cell preparing for my visit, shaping myself up with the razor, when the guard came to my cell to inform me that I had court that morning and they were waiting on me. I wasn't scheduled for court that morning as far as I knew.

I was escorted down to the ground floor, where I went through the normal routine of being handcuffed and shackled.

The Marshals drove me to another building, but to my knowledge, it damn sure wasn't no courthouse! I was escorted to yet another fucking holding cell. I was brought lunch and shortly after, that familiar face was standing out in front of the cell telling me to *cuff up*. No words were exchanged between us as we walked.

I know that whatever was going on, I damn sure wasn't on my way to court!

My eyes grew wide as we entered the room! A room filled with a desk and a stack of folders and pictures spread all across it. That's not why my eyes were wide though! Behind the desk was a tall white man in a suit and at his side, I saw what I had been longing to see for a long time. My baby girl, *Victoria*, sat at his side with her head down. *What the fuck were these people trying to do? Had she been arrested?* They were most likely trying to indict her in order to have leverage on me. They definitely went for my jugular because I would plead in a minute to keep her out of harm's way. I fucked up and she had nothing to do with anything!

"Baby, you alright?" I asked.

She raised her head and lowered it, trying to avoid any eye contact with me. At that moment, that familiar faced muthafucka stood behind her and placed both his hands on her shoulders and looked towards me for a reaction. I sat there and it all came to me now!

That was the same muthafucka with the beat down Expo' at my house that I paid a G to! Only he was cleaner in his three-piece button down suit, with a clean shave! He cleaned up real good!

I screamed out..."You that muthafucka from my house!"

He smiled and said, "You're very perceptive, but it's a little too late for that, don't you think? By the way, Agent Hughes, F.B.I. at your service!"

I was stuck on stupid for a minute when he said, "This here," he said referring to the white man, "is Chief Prosecutor Joseph Waldron, and I don't believe you've been formally introduced. Anthony Fennell, I'd like you to meet Special Agent Cynthia Hodgrin, also known as Victoria Riley."

I couldn't take my eyes off of her! She couldn't meet mine with hers! There was no pain that I've ever felt in my life that could define what I felt at that very moment!

"Excuse me?" I said.

"Well, I guess if anything, we do owe you or better yet, you deserve some kind of explanation."

I checked to make sure the restraints on me were work-

ing properly because I wanted to jump up and kill everything in the room. Especially Victoria or whatever the fuck
her name was!

"Cynthia, huh? Well I guess you did a good job! What
did you get, a fuckin' plaque or something? Was it worth
it?"

She looked up at me with tears in her eyes and said two
words that I'll never forget if I live to be a hundred. She, *this
bitch*, had the audacity to part her lips and say..."I'm sorry!"

"Are you serious? I'm sorry! You're the best, no, the greatest actor to ever grace the earth and the best you could come
up with is *I'm sorry*? When did comedy become your strong
point?" I was so mad that I couldn't even react the way I
wanted to! I wanted to spit in her fuckin' face! Who would
have guessed the devil really wore a dress!

After a minute of silence, this white cat stood from his
seat and said, "As nice as it would be to sit here and enter-
tain this soap opera scenario, some of us do have a job to do
so, if it's an explanation you want...then that's what you'll get,
but when it's all explained to you, take into consideration
that only the people in this room can make your situation
easier *or* harder to deal with! The choice is ultimately yours,
but my question to you is, how much do you actually value
your life?" He went on and said, "Like I said, take your time
and decide, but choose wisely! Alright everybody, where do
we begin?"

They talked and talked and I listened intently, the whole
time staring at this bitch! The whole situation was fucked up!
Evidently these muthafuckas had been on J.O. and X for a
while and I was the key to bringing them down. This broad
wrote me out of nowhere and I assumed it was because I
had my handle on the Internet. My being short in time and
coming up for parole was real convenient. They were the
ones who had me sent to that drug program/halfway house,

knowing it wouldn't be but a matter of time before I escaped. In the process, I would turn to J.O. more than X, because, according to them, he owed me and everything from there played itself out to a tee! I was a pawn in a game of chess! Only they weren't expecting me to come home and take control of things. The murders were a plus! When X was murdered, I was promoted from a pawn to the focus of their investigation, but still a pawn!

They knew everything, some things I had actually forgotten about. They knew where I was this whole time, and exercised their power by telling the state to back off. The bodies were the only thing that were a puzzle to them and my connect, but they knew about the bodies enough to indict me and they knew for a fact that I was the key to the coke being moved! After my conversation with this nigga J.O., it was no longer a puzzle as to who or even why! Pressure bust pipes!

He blew.

They laid a plea on the line that consisted of a life sentence with no chance of parole.

I was fucked up behind this whole thing, but this was life. What had my mind fucked all around was Victoria. I looked at everybody in the room as they waited with anticipation for my response.

"I'll accept the plea!" I said.

"I told you he was a smart man, Joe," the black agent said.

Victoria, well, Agent Hodgrin, jerked her head up in amazement when she heard me agree to a plea. She couldn't believe I was giving in so easily, and she shouldn't have. I spoke again and said, "Under one circumstance." They all stared at me.

"And what exactly would that be, Mr. Fennell?" asked the prosecutor.

I almost laughed as he addressed me as *Mr.* Where the hell did all this fake ass respect come from?

"It's like this here. I'm not a foolish man by far, regardless of my present circumstances, and I believe that every man *and* woman..." I stared real hard and intently at this female rat and continued, "...should and will be held accountable for the things that they do, so I'll save you all the time, money and effort put into a long drawn out trial, but there won't be no testimony coming from me 'cause unlike some people, snake and rat don't dwell in my blood, so my terms are simple. I want these handcuffs and shackles removed and I want thirty minutes in this room alone with *Officer, Agent, Victoria, Cynthia*, whatever her name is!"

"Now you know that's not possible," the prosecutor said.

"Well, those are my terms! Other than that, I'll see you in court and the next time you come up with a stupid ass plea, keep it to yourself, or agree to my terms!"

It wasn't long before they realized this was a waste of a trip and conversation. I was held in that cell for close to six hours. Later I was transported back to the detention center.

Something had to come of this. That whole situation with me and her had to be some form of entrapment. I felt like a sucka! I was!

Chapter Fifteen
Checkmate

The next few months were the longest of my life. I had gotten word from Trini that he would do his best to make a lack of witnesses a priority!

I sent a message through Kia when she came to see me. She was to get my numbers printed out of my phone and find one that the first three digits began with *248* and ask for the *other hand* and inform them that you were calling on the strength of *Jahaad* and tell them that I was in a fucked up situation and I wanted to cash in on that favor promised to me. I told her..."Make sure you tell them I will address a card to the P.O. box and on the inside of the envelope, not the card, will be a name and a figure."

"What P.O. box? What's the address?" she asked.

"Don't worry about that, they'll already know," I responded.

I had prepared for certain things in the town. They possess a key to a post office box and I do to!

Me and Kia were getting real close. She was the support any man in a foul situation would crave. We became friends!

I spoke to her two days after the visit and she informed me that she talked to them and they were waiting for me. That was the best news I heard in a while other than hearing that my daughter took her first steps!

I hurried to my cell and began to prepare the card. Happy birthday was my first choice until I remembered that the chaplain had passed out some sympathy cards. I had kept them for a reason! I hoped to one day be in a position to be able to use each and every one of them! I sent my condolences in the card and on the inside of the envelope in light pencil, I wrote two names and beside them I wrote, *1.5 Mil.*

What good was money if you didn't spend it on the things in life that brought you joy!

I had Kia cop me a subscription to the newspaper in the town so I would be able to get my answer. I read the paper every day religiously!

Two weeks had passed and my trial was set. One month and I would know my fate.

I had my name called at mail call and it wasn't unusual for me to receive mail or anything, but this letter wasn't usual! There was no return address and it was typed and addressed to me. I went back to my cell and sat on my bunk as I began to read...

Dear Anthony,

It is with regret that I write this letter to you under these circumstances. I know that you are doing as well as one can, given the situation. I ask God every night for the above!

I believe that every man and woman will be judged and held accountable for the mistakes they make, but in the end, I believe with all my heart that each individual will be judged by God and it will be done by substance of their heart! We all make our fair share of bad choices, afraid to follow our hearts!

I never wanted that to be the case with you! I was afraid to love you, but you made it close to impossible to not love you. It wasn't supposed to happen, but it did and I have no regrets, other than my inability to be completely honest with you. You may not believe in yourself, but I believe in you. I know this may be worth nothing at this point, but for what it's worth, I was in the process of telling you who I was according to a piece of paper (my birth certificate) and my career. Neither of the two define who I am! You know me better than I've ever known myself, and I will never forgive myself for not having enough courage to tell you before it was too late. Neither do I expect you to be able to forgive me. All that I ask is that you read my words with understanding, for they represent my heart...pieces...small chunks of me!

You gave life to a part of me that I never knew existed and planted seeds in me mentally and emotionally that have grown and blossomed inside of me, and my heart at the present, is the result of that!

Please forgive me, Anthony. I never meant to hurt you! I was afraid to lose you and I gambled with your livelihood for selfish reasons! I believed with all my heart that we could get through this, but the time just never seemed right to tell you. It's not easy to say I love you and in the same conversation say something that has the potential to come between that love! You may never forgive me and to be truthful, I have to respect that, but I will never be denied the love I have for you and I will never accept that you don't love me!

Today, I did what I should have done so long ago! I resigned from my job and I know that doesn't make anything right, but I will spend the rest of my life attempting to! I can't explain the pain I felt to have had to see you chained up like an animal, knowing that I played a role in your being there! You are my sunshine, and without you, my life is full of darkness.

In life there are many things that are inevitable. The sun will rise and set, the tides of the ocean will come in and go back out, the seasons will change, and I will always love and adore you!

I love you more than anything my mind or yours could acknowledge as a comparison to the purest sense of joy! I assure you that I will not be on any witness stand! If I could trade places with you, God knows I would...FORGIVE ME!!!!
LOVING YOU EMPHATICALLY

VICTORIA
What was I supposed to do? There could never be anything between the two of us. I wanted to respond and then I didn't. She left a post office box address under the name Victoria Riley.

I guess she expected me to get emotional and run to a paper and pad and get right at her because her words were so touching and sincere. Was I that much of a fuckin' sucka? Here I was, facing a life sentence, *LIFE*, the rest of my natural life behind a wall or maybe a fence or fences, no more nothing, being told what to do, how to do it and when to do it! A lifetime of seeing or hoping to be able to see and watch my daughter grow up through visits and phone calls. A lifetime of being surrounded by men, some unworthy of the title, and having to lust off of big fat, out of shape cigarette smoking, country, foul attitude bitches! A lifetime of doing my best to abide by the rules and regulations of whatever prison or prisons they choose to send me to across the United States! A lifetime of repetition and loneliness!

Yeah, she definitely knew me better than I thought! She knew it would be close to impossible for me to allow her to have the last and final word and say so, and like the sucka she expected me to be, I reached for a pad and pen and sat there stuck on stupid for the longest time. I had begun a letter maybe twenty times, and each time, deciding against my intro, I crumpled the papers into balls. It wasn't until I took a look around the cell and noticed how foolish that shit must have looked or seemed, that I decided it just wasn't gonna happen. Not now! Not today!

That night, they brought a new batch of inmates up to the block I was on, the same way they did every single day. Or at least that's how it seemed to me. I stood out on the railing and posted up and there were four niggaz brought up! I took a better look, having gotten caught up in the normal routine of the average prisoner worrying about who came up, everybody in search of a homeboy that they knew was at least from their home so they could walk around and kick it with a nigga and talk about people they knew or know and bitches, and hear the latest news. The papers were one thing, but there was nobody that could give you what's really going on better than a nigga from your hood! Besides, niggaz took claim to a muthafucka from their home like they were the best friends on the bricks and they probably didn't even know the nigga. It was crazy, but most cats would play big boy and when one of they mans would show, they would break their backs to make sure the new cat knew the rules of the detention center according to the policy and also to make a point to walk a nigga around and in the process, speak to everyone like they were a major figure in the Feds! Real comical characters!

It's funny how two men will embrace one another as friends simply because you and that individual lived in the same city. I never did understand how a man could be judged by geographical standards! A sucka is a sucka no matter where his mother chose to have him. Real recognized real worldwide!

That geographical shit was for niggaz who ain't ever been nowhere and who were afraid to explore the traveling game. Most muthafuckas fear what they don't know or understand, so they cling to the common and that's not healthy. I learned one thing on my last bid, and that's that it's good to know people from all walks of life and a man should always be judged by his character.

I saw a familiar face as I watched these four niggaz standing by the guard's office. I wasn't completely sure until they were being directed toward their cells. He didn't recognize me at first 'cause I had cut my braids and had gained a little weight.

"Ka, what's good, homie?" I said as he walked by me.

When he turned around and recognized me, he smiled 'cause it's always good to see a familiar face.

"Ant, what up, baby?" he responded.

"I can't call it, man. Shit went south for a nigga."

"Yeah, I heard! How long you been here?" he asked.

"A minute! I see these crackas got you caught up."

Komplete, A.K.A. *Ka* was a young thorough nigga. He was about his work. He ain't work for nobody and he damn sure wasn't fucking with the drug game. He played with them bangers and rented his services out to the highest bidder. His business consisted of him and the twins, Isaiah and Ezekiel, A.K.A. I&E. They basically held niggaz down while they did they thing and guaranteed a drought in beef! Niggaz might not have been feeling the fact that they wasn't on *one* team, but they showed respect to them if only out of fear of some drama!

"Yo, caught up ain't the word, fam! It ain't these crackas at all. It's them coward ass niggaz! Me and *I* was brought in together on this one, but it ain't nothing that can't be fixed. Damn, my bad homie, I been sitting here hollering at you and I ain't even pay my respects."

"Respects for what?" I asked.

"Ya man, Cypher, J.O."

"What about him?"

"Don't tell me you ain't heard yet," he said almost as if he felt bad about what he had to say and I was getting frustrated.

"Dig, homie, what about the nigga?"

"Man, somebody caught him slipping on Saturday and helped him fall. The news said he had got shot multiple times, but word on the street is that he got hit about forty some'em times. That's crazy!"

How the fuck did I miss that shit? Maybe I was looking a little too hard, anticipating, or maybe that letter just had me preoccupied mentally. It didn't even matter 'cause I was happy and at the same time, angry that I couldn't do it.

I hadn't responded to Ka so he said, "I hate to be the bearer of bad news, Ant. I thought you knew, homie."

"Nah! I ain't know, but good looking though," I said.

I helped him get settled in and hit him with some commissary and cigarettes before I went on about my business in search of last week's papers. I had passed them on to an old-head from down my end and I went to get them back. Luckily, I caught him just in time because he was in the process of cleaning his cell. I grabbed the papers and walked to my cell and flipped through them one by one until I got to Sunday's paper. There it was, no picture, just an article titled *Man Slain in Home*.

The papers said he died from multiple gunshot wounds to his head and torso. They were curious as to how something like this could happen in such an upscale neighborhood. Drugs remained a question and police were searching. No suspects or witnesses had been found as of the present! Also that he had most recently been indicted with twelve others!

I felt good, like a burden had been lifted up off of me! I felt great!

Ka showed up at my cell door after count, and I wasn't in the mood to be on no buddy system, but I knew it was gonna happen so I invited him in and basically hipped him to his surroundings and how to deal with these niggaz.

"Trust no one! Everybody wants to help themselves and it's best to keep niggaz at arm's length. Niggaz will try to play you close and if you open a door thinking a mutha-fucka is harmless, it's gonna be hard to close once you find out otherwise and believe me dog, it ain't worth finding out the hard way!"

We sat there and built for a while and time flew by while we went to the bricks. I spent most of the night in my cell, glad that I didn't have a cellmate because there's no better company than yourself sometimes and this was one of those times.

I couldn't sleep and I began to wonder if the second name had been dealt with! I sat down on my bunk and allowed myself to write that letter to her.

(   ),

I chose to leave your name blank because the woman I once knew no longer exists in my world. Besides, I actually have no idea of who you are. I pride myself on my ability to be forward and direct, so I wanna take this opportunity to do just that.

Life is a game of chess and we're all pieces, regardless of our social or financial status, and each individual is most definitely held accountable for their mistakes. You've created a false illusion of "Love" between the two of us, which defies all logic, because we are on opposite sides of the board! You've contributed towards placing me in harm's way and it's necessary for me to make my next choice the best choice because it will effect the rest of the game and although you have placed me in "check," the game is hardly over!

Your letter was received and at one point in time, I may have allowed myself to respond with words full of emotion, but due to a most recent learning experience, that time, as well as that part of me, no longer exists!

The difference between you and myself is that I truly respect the game itself! Meaning, I would never allow my emotions to dictate my next move, unlike yourself. You were unworthy of your position! To be more specific, you are unworthy of the beats of your heart that allow your body to function properly. A waste of flesh (so to speak)!

Any illusions you've created in your mind concerning "Love" between the two of us is and never will be a reality!

You've proven to be scum of the earth and being in a mental and emotional state of confusion, there's no limit to your madness! I will say that, regardless of the circumstances, you were a pleasure, but all good things established on shaky ground are destined for destruction. "It's inevitable."

Forgiveness is unnecessary because it would never change the reality that I'm forced to deal with! You've opened my eyes and for that, I do thank you! I had my blood tested recently and according to the medical staff here at the institution, having read my paperwork concerning those test results, "I'm not alive" because my temperature shows that there is nothing but ice running through my veins.

And so I will remain mentally and emotionally Cold as Ice!
Anthony

First thing in the morning, after breaking night, I rushed the letter to the box to insure that it would be sent out that morning! I didn't want to be left with the option of changing my mind!

I was most definitely gonna have the last and final word! The thing that bothered me was that I was hurt! I was still in love with Victoria, and I didn't know how to stop regardless of anything. My life truly felt incomplete without her and I was ashamed of myself for feeling that way! It was much easier said than done! Believe me! Anyone who would claim otherwise could never have genuinely experienced "Love."

I wanted to mean every single word I wrote to her, but I

didn't. I wanted to write to her and tell her how I felt for real. I even wanted to forgive her! I wanted to understand and most importantly, I wanted to believe!

My pride wouldn't allow me to do that and as hard as it seemed, I know in my heart that it was for the best. She crossed me and still till this day, I never told anybody what happened between us for two reasons. One being, I never wanted to be pegged a fool. Father-Born, may he rest in peace, was right! Two, because I hated myself for it, but I was still trying to be considerate of her feelings and protect her like I always promised to do.

Today was a normal day. Everything was routine and as I sat in the dayroom watching the six o'clock news...

"Early this morning, September 13, 2005, an ex-Federal agent, Cynthia Hodgrin, was brutally gunned down in what witnesses say was 'in the fashion of a bloody and dramatic movie scene.' There have been no comments from the F.B.I. themselves concerning her death or the investigation. According to very few witnesses, two masked men unleashed a hail of gunfire on the unarmed ex-Federal agent..."

I couldn't listen anymore! I felt lost and somehow found my way to my cell. I lay there on my back and felt like a part of me had died! I wished I could take it back, but my wishes never came true and those that have, turned out to be foolish hopes!

It was done and I couldn't do anything about it! I was powerless!

I was placed in *check,* and there was only one option available. I pushed my knights forward to protect myself and as much as I loved her, I had no choice but to place her in *CHECK MATE!* THE GAME WAS OVER!

THE QUESTION IS...*WHO REALLY WON?*

Fan Mail Page

If you have any further questions, comments or concerns, kindly address your inquires in care of:

Michael Whitby

At

AMIAYA ENTERTAINMENT
P.O.BOX 1275
NEW YORK, NY 10159

tanianunez79@hotmail.com

Coming Soon

From
Amiaya Entertainment LLC

"HOEZETTA"
by
Vincent "V. I." Warren

"SO MANY TEARS"
by
Teresa Aviles

www.amiayaentertainment.com

Flower's Bed

Flower's Bed in an incredible tale of a young lady who over-comes her adversities by experiencing pain, understanding real-ity and surrendering to love. At nine years old, Flower Abrams is as innocent as she was when she was first born. Cared for by both her loving mother and deceitful father, tragedy strikes this young child at an age where teddy bears and lollipops can past for best friends and lunch. Emotionally and psychologi-cally affected by this malicious and brutal attack, flower turned to the one thing that brought her solace...the streets.

Flower's Bed

The Most Controversial Book Of This Era

Written By

Antoine "Inch" Thomas

Suspenseful...Fastpaced...Richly Textured

PUBLISHED BY AMIAYA ENTERTAINMENT

No Regrets

Anthony Wheeler is no different from thousands of poor children growing up in his Bronx housing project. He is being raised by a single mother, as are his two bests friends Dev and Slick, and life for them is as normal as it can be in a housing project under the cloud of violence, drugs and constant murders. But then Anthony goes to visit a relative one day and stumbles onto something that changes his life forever. He is intoxicated by the dreamlike lure of fast money and immediate success that the underworld and drug trafficking offers. He plunges head-on into it and spirals downward to the commission of a crime that could land him in jail for the remainder of his life. Like many of his mates, being in prison forces Anthony to have second thoughts about the path he has chosen. Once the doors clang shut behind him. But, unlike the others, instead of this revelation coming over time, Anthony's metamorphosis happens almost immediately after he is incarcerated. He says he has "No Regrets," but there is a distinctive plaintiveness in the voice echoing in his head about the path he has chosen. He seeks redemption by saying over and over to himself, "Only God can judge me."

Unwilling to Suffer

Stephanie Manning is a Stunningly beautiful woman with the brains to match her incredible physical gifts. But, with all she has going for her, she has a problemshe's saddled with a husband, Darryl, who can't contain himself in the presence of other beautiful women.

Blinded by love, Stephanie at first denies there was a problem, until one day her husband's blatant infidelity catches up with him, and all hell breaks loose. The marriage crumbles, the couple separates and Stephanie files for divorce, but that's just the beginning of the madness.

Darryl finds himself caught up in more and more bizarre situations with other women while Stephanie tries her best to keep it all together. She is approached by a young thug in the 'hood and becomes engulfed in a baffling sea of emotions as she is drawn into the young man's romantic web.

Will Stephanie's and Darryl's relationship survive, or will Stephanie succumb to the young thug's advances? Find out in this enchanting and engaging story if stephanie is able to avoid being drawn into a world of sex, drama and violence.

That Gangsta Sh!t

That Gangsta Sh!t is an anthology which features "Inch", as well as several other authors. Each author will mesmerize readers as they journey through the suspense and harsh realities that are a few of the reluctant foundations of life. These shocking tales will fascinate, so much that readers won't be able to close the book.

A Diamond in the Rough

A Diamond in the Rough is the compelling tale of Diamond Weatherspoon's life growing up in the ghetto neighborhoods of Brooklyn, NY. Diamond witnesses her mother Angel, who is 15 years her senior, abused and mistreated by her father Rahmel, a womanizer and major player in the lucrative crack game. When Diamond's mother finally summons up the courage to leave Rahmel, she and Diamond are forced to go on public assistance. Already abused and battered in spirit, Diamond and Angel find themselves living in a woman's shelter until the welfare system can find them adequate housing. Diamond's plans of going to college are interrupted and her dreams of a better life deferred.

Shaped by a life of pain and disappointments, Diamond turns to the Brooklyn streets for refuge. Embracing the shiesty lifestyle of the hustlers in pursuit of the easy life, Diamond encounters many types of people. When she meets Shymeek, an up and coming music producer, the dark hell she calls life begins to look brighter. Finally, Diamond has some breathing room. But things are not always what they seem. Life can change drastically at any moment. Journey into the world of Diamond Witherspoon whose story mirrors so many of our young women that are caught up in the chase for a better life. *A Diamond in the Rough* is a stark reminder that in every city neighborhood there is a rough jewel waiting to be polished to brilliance.

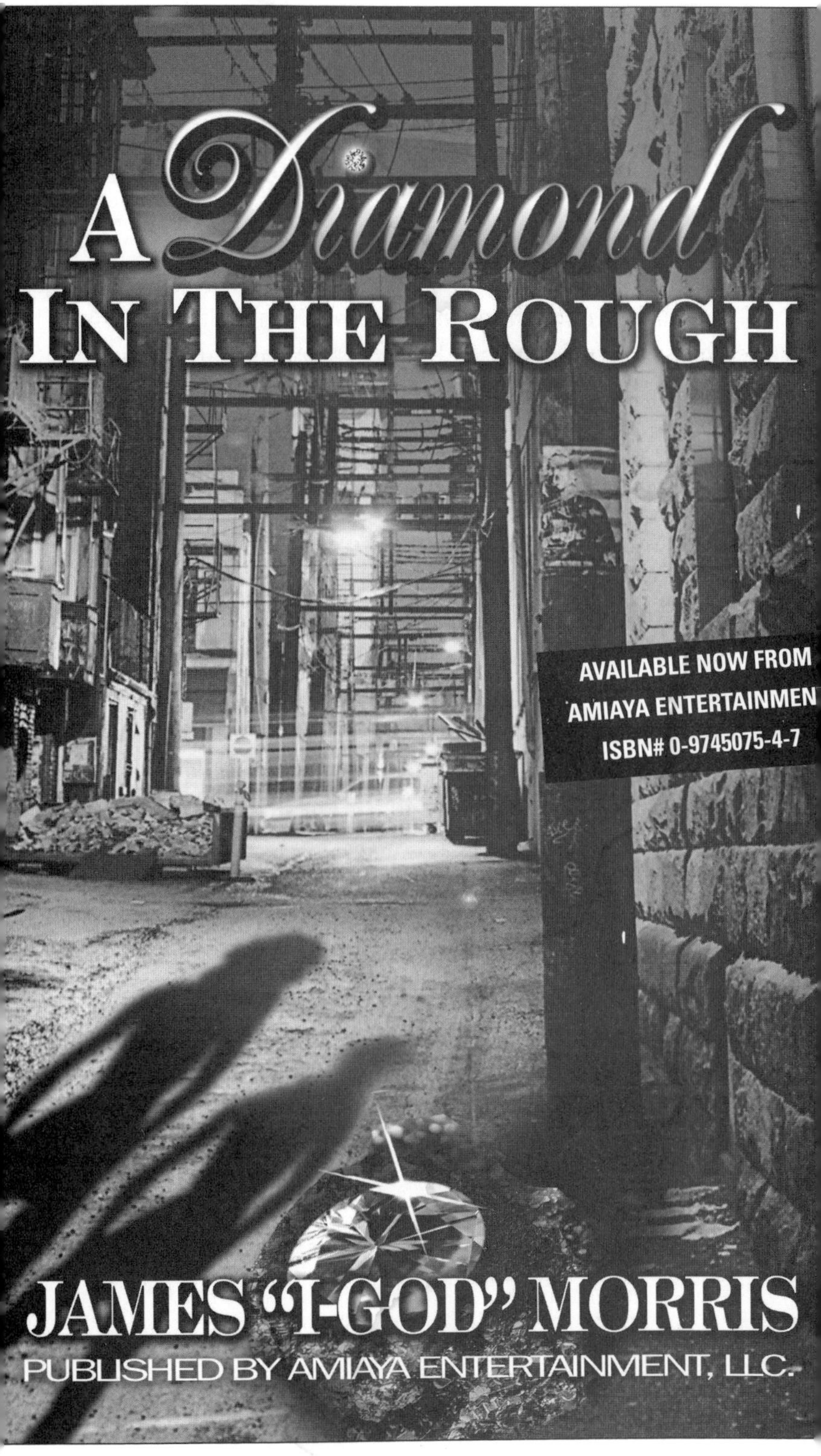
A Diamond
In The Rough
AVAILABLE NOW FROM
AMIAYA ENTERTAINMEN
ISBN# 0-9745075-4-7
JAMES 'I-GOD' MORRIS
PUBLISHED BY AMIAYA ENTERTAINMENT, LLC.

I Aint Mad At Ya

Anthony "Ant" Fennel was born with the will to survive, by any means necessary. In his world, murder and mayhem are facts of life. In a crucial moment, difficult choices are made and consequences can be severe. Ant comes to understand this harsh reality, as he finds himself incarcerated at the age of 15. After serving 6 1/2 of a 7-1/2 to 15-year sentence in the belly of the beast, Ant knows first hand that when it comes to murder, "One is too many, and a thousand is never enough."

Once released from prison, Ant returns to the infamous life style that had previously consumed him. For a short time he's at the top of the game. But it's truly a lonely place at the top. Murder, madness and money don't make for good friendships. Friends are hard to come by. Who can a brother trust? Are money and the heinous things that come along with it worth the nightmare ride?

Join Ant on his quest to find the answers to these questions and in the process possibly discover the meaning of manhood. See how one young man comes to understand that when it comes to the "game" there is only one rule. Only the strong survive!

TRAVIS "UNIQUE" STEVENS

AVAILABLE NOW FROM
AMIAYA ENTERTAINMENT
ISBN# 0-9745075-5-5

I AIN'T MAD AT ya

PUBLISHED BY AMIAYA ENTERTAINMENT, LLC.

Against the Grain

Boo and Moe are brothers who's father died of a drug overdose when they were very young. Raised by a tough mother and her new companion Rufus, the boys grow up to be street-wise, hardened individuals who eventually form their neighborhood's toughest street gang. Toughness was their gang's mantra, and was reflected in their chosen name -- B.M.F., for Bad Mutha Fuckas.

But the brothers were also clever enough to know that all brawn and no brains would eventually spell their doom, so they turned to Rufus for guidance. It was a smart move, because Rufus soon had the rough BMFs drug dealings operating like a well managed organization.

Boo was the brains and Moe was the brawn, and they were a formidable combination that soon was recognized by all the other gangs as top dogs. Boo and Moe owned the streets of their neighborhood.

At this point Johnson takes another turn in his story telling. He makes Boo befriend a young man named Steve who's mother is a heroin addict, and adds another element to Boo's personality by giving him the compassion and the insight to transform himself into Steve's unoffcial mentor. Boo loves Steve so much he asks him to be his newborn son's Godfather.

Everything was fine until Steve brings his cousin Reno into the gang family, and that's when the chaos begins, because Reno is not exactly the sit-back type. Steve soon is caught in the middle of an increasingly deadly power struggle between Boo, Moe and Reno.

Altercations and confrontations occur more frequently each day, so much so that Steve finally admits to himself that he has to make a choice.

At this point, Johnson again adds another twist. Did Boo and Moe think they had enough troubles with Reno? Well, when Boo negotiates with a new drug supplier, here comes one of those rival bad boys from their past who's either jealous or frustrated or both, and off we go again.....

A STORY THAT WILL HAVE YOU ON YOUR TOES FROM BEGINING TO END...

AGAINST THE GRAIN

AVAILABLE NOW FRO

AMIAYA ENTERTAINMI

ISBN# 0-9745075-6-3

G.B. JOHNSON

PUBLISHED BY AMIAYA ENTERTAINMENT, LLC.

All Or Nothing

ORDER FORM

Number of Copies

All Or Nothing	ISBN# 0-9745075-7-1	$15.00/Copy	_____
Against The Grain	ISBN# 0-9745075-6-3	$15.00/Copy	_____
Ain't Mad At Ya	ISBN# 0-9745075-5-5	$15.00/Copy	_____
Diamonds In The Rough	ISBN# 0-9745075-4-7	$15.00/Copy	_____
Flower's Bed	ISBN# 0-9745075-0-4	$14.95/Copy	_____
That Gangsta Sh!t	ISBN# 0-9745075-3-9	$15.00/Copy	_____
No Regrets	ISBN# 0-9745075-1-2	$15.00/Copy	_____
Unwilling To Suffer	ISBN# 0-9745075-2-0	$15.00/Copy	_____

PRIORITY POSTAGE (4-6 DAYS US MAIL): Add $4.95

Accepted form of Payments: Institutional Checks or Money Orders

(All Postal rates are subject to change.)

Please check with your local Post Office for change of rate and schedules.

Please Provide Us With Your Mailing Information:

Billing Address_____

Name: _____

Address:_____

Suite/Apartment#: _____

City:_____

Zip Code:_____

Shipping Address

Name:_____

Address:_____

Suite/Apartment#:_____

City:_____

Zip Code:_____

(Federal & State Prisoners, Please include your Inmate Registration Number)

Send Checks or Money Orders to:
AMIAYA ENTERTAINMENT
P.O.BOX 1275
NEW YORK, NY 10159
212-946-6565

www.amiayaentertainment.com